Capturing Peace

Also by Molly McAdams

Deceiving Lies
Needing Her (Novella)
Forgiving Lies
Stealing Harper (Novella)
From Ashes
Taking Chances

Capturing Peace

A NOVELLA

MOLLY McADAMS

WILLIAM MORROW IMPULSE
An Imprint of HarperCollinsPublishers

Excerpt from *Sharing You* copyright © 2014 by Molly Jester.
Excerpt from *Forgiving Lies* copyright © 2013 by Molly Jester.

EPub Edition APRIL 2014 ISBN: 9780062300133
Print Edition ISBN: 9780062300140

10 9 8 7 6 5 4 3 2 1

For Tyler: Your life is much more interesting than you know.

Capturing Peace

Prologue

Reagan—*January 3, 2004*

ALL THE AIR left my body in a hard rush. It felt like my stomach was on fire and simultaneously dropping . . . it felt like my heart was being torn from my chest.

No. No, I must have heard him wrong. He didn't just say that to me.

"W-what? Austin, what did you say?" My voice came out barely above a whisper.

Austin looked around us, the set of his face was hard, and so unlike anything I'd ever seen from him. He was always smiling, laughing, joking . . . not this. Never this. He was the quarterback of the varsity football team; he was one of the most popular guys in our school. Everyone loved him and his easygoing— somewhat cocky—attitude. I loved him . . . he loved me. I knew he did, he couldn't be doing this to me.

Leaning in, his blue eyes darted around us again one last time before he whispered, "I said, get rid of it."

One hand flew to my mouth to muffle the shocked cry that had just left me, the other went to my stomach. "No, don't say that to me." Tears streamed quickly down my face. I'd been afraid too when I had first realized I was pregnant; I kept telling myself all Austin needed was some time to get used to the idea. "I know we're young, but we can do this together, I know we can."

"Reagan, I'm sixteen!" he growled into my ear. "I'm not about to have a motherfucking kid. Get rid of it."

My head shook back and forth slowly. "Austin—"

"I'm not gonna let you ruin both our futures. We have two and a half years of high school left, they were already scouting me this last season, Ray. Do you know how rare that is for a sophomore? Do you know how big of a deal it is for me to already be the varsity QB? I'm not letting you fuck this up for me. Get. Rid. Of it."

"No!" I shouted, and slapped at his hands when he reached for my arms. "No! I can't—I can't believe you'd even ask me to do something like that. I know it's scary, baby, I'm terrified. But we'll get through it together; I *need* you. I can't go through this alone."

"Reagan . . . I'm not asking you. I'm telling you. Get rid of it, or we're done."

Another choked sob tore through me, and my hands dropped down to my stomach.

"Jesus, will you stop?" he hissed, and pulled my hands back so they were at my sides. "Everyone can hear you, and when you do shit like that, they're gonna figure out what's happening."

It was the end of the first day back from winter break, there were only a handful of people still at the school, and none of them were near us. I'd been trying to figure out how to tell Austin all throughout break, and hoped that he'd help me find a way to tell my parents. Hoped that I'd be able to take refuge at school if they didn't take the news well.

I'd been wrong.

I stood there staring at his hardened features for a few minutes before backing away from his grasp. "I can't get rid of the baby. I won't."

"You're screwing with your future, Ray, think about that. That thing"—his nostrils flared, and lips curled as the word left him—"is not a damn baby yet. Last chance . . . I'm not going to tell you again."

He called our baby a thing. A thing!

I didn't know how far along I was since I didn't pay attention to my cycles, which were never on time anyway. Something my family doctor said probably had to do with my dancing and cheerleading. I hadn't had any morning sickness; and it hadn't been until my cheer skirt stopped fitting, and the captain of our team told me I should start eating less, that I'd even thought I could be pregnant. By the time I'd gotten over the denial, gained the courage to even buy and take a test—or five—and gotten over the denial again, I was already sporting a small bump on my otherwise flat and toned stomach. A bump proving there was a life growing inside me . . . not a *thing*.

Squaring my shoulders, I ignored the tears still falling and my quivering chin, and looked directly into Austin's blue eyes. "I'm keeping the baby."

A look of shock crossed his face for all of two seconds before he was glaring at me again. "Just remember: You're the one who threw us away. You're the one ruining your life. Try to bring me down with you, and I'll say that thing isn't mine."

Locking my jaw, I refused to give him the satisfaction of seeing how much this was killing me. How much I wanted to beg him not to do this. Well, more than I'd already shown. I knew he was hoping his ultimatum would change my mind, and nothing could at this point.

His eyes searched mine for a few more seconds before he straightened with a huff. "Fuck it. Good-bye, Reagan."

I watched him walk away toward the parking lot, his head turning to each side to see who'd witnessed our conversation. Once his shiny black Camaro peeled out of the lot, I finally unlocked my knees and somehow made my way to my car.

I didn't remember the drive back to my house. I didn't remember climbing the stairs to my room. The next thing I knew, I was in my bathroom with my shirt pulled up, my yoga pants pushed down a little, and my hands were gently running over my stomach when a gasp sounded behind me.

My head snapped up before I whirled around to see my mom standing there. Even through my blurred vision from the tears, I could see her standing there, her head shaking back and forth, her hands over her mouth.

"No . . . Reagan, no!"

I burst into strained sobs, unable to try and brush it off as something else. My boyfriend of the last eighteen months had just broken my heart. He'd called our baby a thing. I'd been stressing over hiding my bump with loose-fitting clothing for almost a month now. I'd only turned sixteen a couple weeks ago and was having a baby.

All the emotions crashed down on me, and no matter how much I wanted to deny it, I needed my mom right then.

"M-mom," I somehow managed to say through the near-hyperventilating crying.

"No. What have you done?" she shrieked as she backed away from me.

"Mom, please!"

I followed her into my bedroom, and our heads turned toward my door when heavy footsteps sounded on the stairs. My older brother burst into my room, quickly followed by my dad.

What is he already doing home? He usually isn't home for another few hours.

I panicked when I saw the look of horror cross both

their faces. Their eyes were glued to my stomach. I quickly pulled my shirt down to cover it, but my arms stayed in front of my little bump, like I was protecting my baby from what was about to happen.

"Daddy," I cried, and started to take a step toward him, but he took one away.

"I'm going to kill him," my brother, Keegan, whispered. "I swear to God I'll kill him."

"What have you done, Reagan?" Mom screamed again.

My chest ached, and the tears somehow—impossibly—fell harder. "Mom, I'm—"

"Tell me you're not pregnant! Damn it, Reagan, tell me!"

Hands gripped my arms just as my knees gave out beneath me. "Stop screaming at her!" Keegan yelled back as he walked me toward my bed. "She's upset enough as it is, you're not helping anything."

When we were sitting, I gripped my brother's hand like a lifeline . . . the only way I could thank him in that moment.

"Did you know this?" Mom turned her attention on Keegan, her voice still shrill. "Did you know this, and you kept it from us?"

"Austin wouldn't be alive if I'd known about this! But you're making this worse, she's probably terrified and you yelling is stressing her out!"

"Don't tell me how to react to this situation! Don't you dare! Get out of the room!"

"Mom, I'm pissed too! I'm forcing myself not to leave this house because I know I'll go hunt Austin down. But we need to calm down for Reagan! If she's pregnant, this isn't going to help the baby."

Mom gripped my desk like she needed it to stay standing. Her voice wavered, but she never stopped screaming. "She can't be pregnant . . . Reagan, you *can't* be pregnant!"

Even though Keegan was trying to calm the room, my dad was the only one who hadn't spoken and wasn't crying. I looked at him, hoping for something from him. Anything. But his eyes were still glued to my stomach. "Dad . . . ?"

He slowly looked up at me, his face still showing how horrified he was. "I can't even look at you right now. You're not my daughter."

"Daddy!" I choked out when he turned and left the room.

"Dad!" Keegan barked, his hold on me tightening.

"Why would you let this happen?"

I looked back to my mom when her softened voice reached me. Somehow, my heart continued to break even more when I saw the disappointment in her eyes.

"This can't be happening," she said, and then turned to quickly leave my room.

I collapsed into Keegan's arms, and was surprised at the force of my next round of sobs. I hadn't expected my family to be happy, but even my worst fears hadn't been prepared for that.

We heard the front door slam shut just a few minutes after Mom had left my room, and from her pleas as she called him over and over again, I knew Dad had left.

"I'M SORRY," I mumbled hours later, when my tears had run dry. Keegan hadn't once left my side. "I'm so sorry."

He kissed the top of my head and hugged me tighter. "*I'm* sorry, Ray. I—I can't believe this either, but you know I'm always here for you. They'll come around, they're just shocked right now."

"They hate me."

"No, they don't. You just need to wait until they process it." I didn't respond, because I didn't believe him. A few minutes later, he asked, "Does Austin know?"

I nodded my head and told him everything that happened that afternoon. I didn't cry again, I wasn't sure if I'd ever be able to cry again. My voice was robotic as I replayed the conversation, and I didn't flinch when Keegan's hard voice swore again that he would kill Austin. I knew he wouldn't, but I had no doubt he would do something.

Keegan held me until I fell asleep on his shoulder from the exhaustion of the day. When I woke, it was dark in my room, but I could still make out my dad's shape as he sat on the edge of my bed, his back to me, one of his hands gripping mine. I didn't move, or give any indication that I'd woken. To be honest, I was afraid of what he'd say to me then.

He hunched in on himself, and his hand tightened around mine. And for the first time in my life, I watched my dad as he cried.

Chapter One

Reagan—*July 23, 2010*

I BENT DOWN to kiss my son's head, straightened, and tiptoed out of his room, shutting the door behind me. Grabbing my phone, I called my mom as I went around the apartment picking up the toys Parker had received for his sixth birthday.

"Hi, sweetheart!"

"Hey, Mom," I huffed as I dropped everything into his toy chest and let the lid shut. "Parker passed out playing."

Her soft laugh filled the phone. "I bet, today was crazy. Did he have fun?"

"Understatement. 'Fun' is an understatement. Thank you for everything you did to help. He really did have a blast, and he *loved* his presents."

"Good, I'm glad. What are you going to do for

the rest of the night? Did you want to come over for brunch tomorrow?"

I smiled as I waited for the next words that would come from her.

"I just hate that you two are so far away."

Laughing, I plopped down on the couch and stretched out. "It's not even a ten-minute drive!"

"But you're all alone, and ten minutes is a long time in case of an emergency."

"Mom, I love you, we're fine. I'm just going to watch TV until I'm tired, and, yes, brunch tomorrow sounds great."

There was a beat of silence before she said, "You're always welcome to bring someone, honey."

I suppressed a groan. I knew she was just looking out for Parker and me, but I didn't need—or want—a man in my life.

There hadn't been anyone since Austin had given me an ultimatum of being together, or keeping Parker. There hadn't been a need for a guy. I knew no one would want a child at my age, and I had my family.

Even though the first day of my family knowing had been intense—well, really, the first month had been—my family had supported my decision to keep the baby, and had been there for me through everything. Keegan had gone to Austin's that first night and beaten the shit out of him. Austin and his parents hadn't pressed charges when Keegan told his parents about our breakup, and Austin hadn't said a word to me since.

I'd continued going to school, and when rumors started flying about my growing belly, Austin told all our friends that I'd cheated on him. He'd taken another beating from Keegan for that, but I never tried to stop the rumors. Like I'd done in our last minutes together, I'd refused to give him the satisfaction of seeing how much he'd hurt me.

I refused to let *anyone* see how much they were hurting me.

With help from my mom, I'd finished out the rest of high school, and graduated with a 3.9 GPA. Even though my parents encouraged me to go to college, I'd decided against it and had immediately begun looking for a job that could support my son and me. I'd started at the bottom of a local business, and had quickly worked my way up over the last four years. Within six months of graduation, Parker and I had moved into the apartment we still lived in, and I'd fought my mom on putting him in day care.

She'd won.

She watched him while I worked, but I paid her just as much as the nicest day care in the city charged. I wasn't stupid, though; I knew she was "secretly" putting the money in a college account for Parker. But Dad had made me promise I wouldn't let on to the fact that I knew, so I'd kept paying her, and Parker had continued going to her house five days a week until he'd gone into kindergarten last year.

My life was perfect. My son was healthy and incredibly smart, he and I both had a great relationship with my parents and brother, and I was supporting us well enough that we lived in a great complex and I could give him whatever he wanted. Eh, well, to an extent. But why mess that up by throwing a guy into the picture?

"Mom, I'm not bringing anyone."

"You need a man in your life . . . *Parker* needs a dad."

Damn it. I hated when she involved Parker . . . she knew how that got to me. "He has Keegan and Dad."

"Keegan only comes home every other weekend if he's not deployed."

Keegan had joined the army after deciding college wasn't for him, two years in. I was so proud of him, and thankful he was stationed only a little over an hour from Denver so he could come home often. "And he's getting out soon, so he'll be around more."

"I know you *can* do this on your own, Reagan. But that doesn't mean you have to or should."

"Dating would be exhausting for me . . . and I don't want to put Parker through that." I chewed on my bottom lip for a second as I debated whether or not I should voice my fears. With a hard breath, I told her the rest quickly. "Austin didn't want him, I wouldn't be able to handle it if I let someone into our life and he decided he didn't want Parker either."

"Reagan," she crooned, her voice wavering. "They won't all be like him."

"I know, I just—I'm not ready for that possibility.

You know? I can take the rejection . . . just not if they reject him."

"I understand, sweetheart. I really do. But I'll never stop praying for the perfect man for you and Parker."

I wanted to tell her that even if he was out there, I probably wouldn't give him the time of day; but the way she was talking broke my heart, so I kept my mouth shut. I knew everyone in my family wanted that for Parker and me, and it's not that I didn't want that for us either. I just couldn't imagine myself taking that leap of faith in someone else. Someone who could potentially ruin us forever.

Coen—*July 30, 2010*

"SACO, MAN, YOU can't let her fucking do this to you. It's your fucking kid, she can't just keep him from you."

"What am I supposed to do? Try to get custody of him from my own wife? I've never even seen him before. I was gone through Liv's pregnancy, the delivery, and for the first three months of his life. No judge is going to grant me custody."

"So you're actually going to listen to her? This is bullshit."

"I know, Steele, but I have no choice. I *need* to be able to see my son. I'm already waiting on this realtor to go look at some places. I'll call you when I have news, yeah?"

"Yeah, all right. Sorry this is happening, man, I really am."

"Me too." An exhausted sigh sounded through the phone. "Later."

I pressed END, and looked over at Hudson. "His bitch wife is making him buy them a house before she'll let him meet their son."

"The fuck?" Hudson balked, and lowered himself into a chair. "Can she do that?"

I shrugged and tossed my phone onto my dresser. "Apparently, because he's meeting with a realtor."

Our friend, Brody Saco, had gotten out of the army not even a week ago. He'd been planning on making this a career, but all that had changed when his girl from back home wound up pregnant. He'd married her immediately, and ever since then, she'd refused to see him or let him meet their son—and it'd been a year since their wedding. I could respect him for taking responsibility, but we all felt bad for him because he'd blindly gone into a shit storm with her.

"What are you doing this weekend?" Hudson asked me, and it was then I noticed his backpack sitting at his feet.

"Got some shoots booked in the area. You heading home?"

He nodded and drummed his hands on the arms of the chair. "Yeah, I missed my nephew's birthday last weekend, I need to go see him and my sister."

"All right, I'll see you when you get back."

"If you don't feel like coming back to base between your shoots, hit me up, you can stay at my parents' place or something."

I laughed and shook my head. "Nah, I'm good. Thanks though."

Hudson stood to leave, but stopped at the door, and a knowing look crossed his face. "Try to get some sleep."

"Uh . . . yeah. I'll do that."

He and I both knew that wouldn't be happening. I was lucky if I got two hours in a night. If I didn't have photos I could edit during those long hours, I would go insane.

Once he was gone, I made sure everything was charged, and packed up all my equipment before heading out to the studio I had in Denver. I had a few photo shoots set up for the night—some with friends, and one with a new client. The shoots, along with the editing and wedding I was covering the next day, would keep me busy throughout the weekend. Busy was how I liked my life. How I preferred it. It kept me from remembering things I wished I'd never seen.

TWO WEEKS LATER, I walked into the room I'd been sharing with Hudson since Saco had gotten out, and stood there staring at everything for a few minutes. Today was bittersweet. It was a day I'd been waiting on for months now, and at the same time, a day I couldn't have prepared for.

I'd been in the army for almost six years, and like Saco, I'd been prepared to make this a career. But with my photography business taking off and demanding more of my time, I'd had to make a decision. The army was all I'd known since I turned eighteen, but in the last year I'd started realizing that photography was more than a hobby; it was my passion.

I thought I wouldn't be getting out for another month or so, but I'd gotten the call this morning and had spent the next handful of hours in an office waiting, and then signing the papers signifying my official retirement. Typical "Hurry up and wait," and then, "Surprise, fucker!" bullshit from the military. Like I should have expected anything else.

Halfway through throwing everything in my bags and moving my camera equipment out to my car, Hudson came back.

"Man, with you and Saco gone, it's gonna be boring as shit until I get out of here too."

"Aww, you're gonna miss me? Touched, bro, really am. But I told you, I don't swing that way," I joked with him as I grabbed more of my stuff.

"Fuck off, Steele. You know what I meant. Whatever, though, I'll be out of here soon."

"Are you going to get a place with your girl?"

Hudson fell onto his bed and stretched out. "Probably, it'd just be easier that way. But I don't know if she really wants to move all the way up to Denver. I mean, I know its not far, but she has a job here, and I need to be close to my sister."

Out of all the things we'd talked about through the years, his sister wasn't one of them. All I knew was if he wasn't sticking around base on the weekends so he could see his girlfriend, he was going home so he could be near his sister and her son. "I've never asked because I figured you'd tell me if you wanted me to know. But what is it with your sister that always has you going home?"

He thought for a few minutes before responding. "Reagan just needs me. She'd never admit that, she's independent and stubborn as shit; but she needs me. We've always been close, but she got pregnant when she was sixteen and her asshole boyfriend told her to have an abortion or he was leaving her."

I snorted. "Dick."

"Yeah. Obviously he's not around anymore; but all her friends ditched her, and she only had our parents and me on her side after that. She's done well for herself and is an awesome mom, but she thinks she has to do this all alone. Like I said, stubborn and independent. The only guys around her son are my dad and me, and he's six now. He needs male role models in his life, you know?"

"Understand. That sucks for her, though."

My mom had had me when she was a teenager as well, but had given me up for adoption as soon as I'd been born. I'd never resented her, because I grew up in a great family . . . and obviously she couldn't have given me that. That didn't stop me from wondering why she hadn't tried. So I was already impressed by Reagan's drive, and I'd never even met her.

"That it does." Hudson's voice interrupted my thoughts. "So, are you moving back home?"

"Ahh, nah. I don't think so. I miss them and all, but I'd miss my studio. I have a lot of clients here who I can keep using, and I'd miss the location. Colorado is a lot nicer to look at and shoot in than where I grew up."

Hudson laughed. "I bet. Well, where are you gonna stay? I know you weren't expecting to get out today."

"I'll just crash in my studio until I find a place, no big deal."

"You sure? I can call one of my buddies."

"Appreciate it, man, but for what? So I can *not* sleep on their couch? I have couches in the studio if I need to pass out."

He looked at me for a few moments before saying, "You should really talk to someone. They could help."

I knew he was looking out for me, but I hated when people said shit like that. I didn't need help. "I have nothing to say to anyone, there's no point."

Sensing my unease with the conversation, Hudson held up his hands like he was surrendering and changed the subject. "Well, your studio is close to where my family is and where I'll be looking for a place when I get out. So let's grab some beers when you're not busy, all right? Actually, I'm heading home this weekend. Want to go out and celebrate your civilian status tonight?"

"Civilian," I huffed, and shook my head. "Fuck,

this is gonna be weird. I don't know if I remember how to be a civilian."

"It'll be easier than you think, I'm sure."

I somehow doubted that. Grabbing the last of my bags, I looked over at him and nodded. "Yeah, let's go out tonight. Call me when you head into the city, I'm gonna take everything to the studio and look at the places around there for a few hours."

"Will do, see you later."

With one last look at the room, I turned and headed out of the barracks to start my new *civilian* life. Jesus Christ, that was going to take some getting used to.

Reagan—*August 13, 2010*

I FINISHED PAYING for my coffee and shoved everything back in my wallet as I answered my phone.

"Hello?"

"Hey, Ray."

Huffing as I jammed my wallet into my purse and tried to get out of the way for the next person waiting to order, I put my phone between my shoulder and my cheek, and sighed. "Hey, big brother."

"You okay?" he asked on a laugh.

"Fine. Today was just the longest day ever, and I barely slept last night, so I feel like I'm about to lose my shit. I'm getting coffee before I go get Parker from Mom."

His next laugh was louder, fuller. "Sounds like you need a beer, not coffee."

"Wouldn't that be nice?" I mused.

"I'm coming home tonight and hitting up a bar with my roommate. He's officially retired as of today, so we're celebrating. Come out with us."

"Thanks, but no. I just want to get Parker and go home."

Keegan sighed, and I mentally prepared myself for what was coming next. Swear to God, my entire family was like one giant broken record. "You need to go out and just relax. One night away from your son isn't going to kill you. I know Mom and Dad will watch him."

"Of course they will, and they'd probably shove me out the door to hang out with you. But I don't want a night away from him."

"Reagan, it's just a few hours. Come hang out with us, have a good time, meet some people . . ."

I gasped as I realized what he was hinting at. "Keegan Hudson, are you trying to set me up with your friends?"

There was a long pause before he admitted, "Yeah, Ray, I am. He's a good guy, I know you'd like him . . . and he's moving close to you. It would be good for him to know someone there."

"Christ, not you too. I don't want to meet anyone, why is that so hard for all of you to understand?"

"Because—"

"This is so backwards! Shouldn't you be keeping

me from guys? Especially your soldier buddies?" I mouthed a thank-you to the barista, and grabbed my iced latte as I turned to leave.

"You know . . . it's not a crime to date."

"I know that, Kee—shit!" I gasped, and jumped back from the iced coffee, even though it was already covering most of my shirt.

"What?" he yelled into the phone. "What happened?"

"Oh my God," the guy in front of me said. His face somewhat apologetic, somewhat amused. "I'm so sorry, are you okay?"

"Reagan! What happened?"

I pulled the shirt away from my body, and stood there in shock for a few seconds before my brain started functioning again. "Nothing, I just *literally* ran into a guy at Starbucks and am now covered in coffee."

"That shit actually happens?" Keegan laughed. "Only you, Ray, only you."

"I'm so sorry," the guy said again. "Please, let me buy you a drink . . . and a new shirt. Shit, here let me get napkins."

Keegan was quiet for a few seconds before he asked, "Who is that with you?" His voice was laced with a curiosity I'd never heard from him.

"I don't know, I've never seen him before."

"Ask him his name."

"No, look, I need to go. I'm soaked and there's coffee all over the ground. I'll talk to you later."

He sighed. "Fine. Call me later, and think about coming out with us. Love you, sis."

"Love you too," I said quietly, and dropped my phone into my already full purse to take the napkins from the guy's hands. He looked like he couldn't decide if he should try to clean me off, or if he should let me do that. So I made the decision for him.

"What did you have? I'll get you another."

I looked up at his face, and tried not to scoff at his amused expression. Watching him until he finally looked up from my damp shirt, I narrowed my eyes at him. "Don't worry about it, this is probably a sign I shouldn't have stopped for coffee."

I'd started bending down to clean up what had made it onto the floor, when he grabbed my arm. My body froze from its descent, and I stared at his full sleeve of black tattoos before slowly looking up at his dark eyes. They were almost black, and held mine captive until his lips moved again. The amusement was gone from his face and tone, his deep voice now gruff as he spoke. "I'll get that, this was my fault."

"I turned into you, it's mine."

"I shouldn't have been standing right behind you."

We looked at each other in silence for a few seconds, before I snapped back to reality. Pulling my arm from his grasp, I took a step back from him and looked away from his intense stare. Clearing my throat, I hitched my purse higher up on my shoulder and searched for a trash can.

"Can I please buy you another drink?"

"No, it's fine. Really."

He laughed awkwardly and looked around for a second. "I'm trying to make up for spilling your drink on you . . . and you're making it really hard."

Squeezing my eyes shut, I took a deep breath in and out before turning back to him. I knew I was coming across as a bitch, but I hated asking for help, and didn't like when people offered it. It's not that I wasn't grateful for people, it was just the idea of not being able to handle a situation by myself left me feeling like I was seconds from panicking.

Offering him a forced smile, I tried to keep the strain out of my voice when I said, "I appreciate your attempt at reminding me that chivalry isn't dead, but I really am fine."

Grabbing his drink off the counter, he offered it to me. "Then will you take mine?"

My next smile wasn't forced. "Thank you, but no."

"You're really going to leave me standing here feeling like an asshole?" I might have felt bad if he wasn't smirking at me.

"I'm sure you'll live. Have a good night," I called over my shoulder as I walked past him.

His hand grasped my elbow, and my breath came out in a soft huff. His hold wasn't menacing, and even though it should bother me to have a stranger touching me, it didn't. But I absolutely refused to think about why my skin felt like it was on fire where he was holding me.

"Can I at least have your name?"

My voice came out breathy, and I silently cursed myself and his dark, mesmerizing eyes. "And why would you want that?"

"Excuse me, miss?"

I looked over at the barista, but from the corner of my eye, I could see the man's eyes still on me.

The barista lifted up an iced latte before setting it down on the counter. "Saw what happened, this is on me."

"Thank you so much," I whispered to her after I pulled away from his hand. I hope she understood just how grateful I was for this. Looking back at the guy, I unnecessarily showed him the new drink and shot him a smile. "Well, I guess that solves that. Thank you for everything anyway. Have a good weekend."

My smile fell and a short huff left me when I began walking away. *What the hell was that, Reagan?* I liked being in control of situations and my emotions, and the longer I stayed in his presence, the more I'd felt myself losing control of all of it.

Reaching for the bar on the door, I felt a warm chest brush against my back at the same time a tattooed arm shot in front of me and pushed the door open.

"So, how about that name?" he asked huskily, and a smile crossed my face as a shiver worked its way through my body.

Turning to look up at him after we were outside, I shrugged and shook my head, but I still couldn't contain the smile on my face. "What good would it do for you to know it?"

"Humor me."

Biting down on my cheek, I raised one shoulder and started walking backward toward my car. "I'm just the girl covered in coffee. Good night."

I was also the girl who couldn't get him out of my mind even hours later, when I got in bed. His short dark hair, near black eyes, cocky smirk, and lean, toned body covered in tattoos were all I could see when I closed my eyes that night.

Coen—*August 13, 2010*

"THERE HE IS," Hudson's voice boomed when I walked over to the table he was sitting at with his girlfriend and a few more people I'd never met before.

I slapped his hand and ordered a beer before the waitress could step away. "Hey, man, sorry I'm late. I had to run back to the studio and change."

He shot me a knowing look, and I wanted to ask what it was for. "How'd apartment hunting go?"

"It didn't. Once I got to my studio, I set up my equipment and did some edits for a while. I went to grab a coffee on my way out, and ended up running into this girl." Hudson's eyebrow lifted and I rolled my eyes. "Not like that, I mean I *ran* into her. Made her spill her coffee all over both of us."

His lips twitched and he covered it by taking a long pull from his beer. "Is that so?" he asked after. "Did you catch her name?"

"Uh . . . no. Wasn't because I didn't try though. Whatever, story of my life."

"Is she hot?"

Hudson's girlfriend, Erica, started laughing, and buried her face in Hudson's shoulder to muffle it. I couldn't understand why she hadn't hit him. She hated when he would bring up other girls.

Why the hell is he acting so weird? "Yeah . . . ? Yeah, she was. Am I missing something?"

Erica snorted and laughed harder. Her shoulders were shaking, and her face turned bright red. "Nope," Hudson said, but he was now full-on grinning. "Maybe you'll see her again."

"I doubt it, I've been going to that Starbucks since I got my studio years ago. Never seen her before." I said each word slowly as I watched Erica fan at her face, and Hudson struggle to contain his smile. *What the fuck did I miss?* "If you don't tell me what the hell is going on, I'm leaving."

The waitress put my beer in front of me, but I didn't touch it as I waited for him to answer.

"Don't leave, we're celebrating," Hudson said at the same time Erica pled, "Aww, Coen, don't leave! Keegan had been telling me a, uh, funny story before you showed up, and I just now got it. You know me . . . just another blond moment."

Erica was a natural brunette.

I stood, but Hudson reached over and pushed me back down. "Stay. I haven't even introduced you to everyone else yet. Let's just have a good night, 'kay?"

"Sure, whatever." Grabbing my beer, my mind was already off Hudson and Erica's odd behavior. Hazel eyes, long blond hair, and a soft smile replaced everything and stayed forefront in my mind for the rest of the night.

Chapter Two

Reagan—*August 15, 2010*

Pulling Parker out of his booster seat, I helped him get out of my SUV and followed him as he ran up my parents' driveway.

Just as I'd been about to remind him to knock first, my dad threw the front door open and grabbed Parker up. Throwing him over his shoulder, he tickled my son's sides for a few seconds before setting him back on the ground.

"Hey, Dad," I said as I kissed his cheek and closed the door behind me.

"Are you staying for a few minutes?"

I made a face and looked at him like he was crazy. "Uh, Mom invited us for lunch today."

"Hi, sweetheart! Are you hanging out here for a bit? I figured you'd be on your way by now," Mom stated as she pulled me in for a hug.

"Wait, what?" I froze as I tried to remember where I was supposed to be today. "I thought I only had lunch with you guys today. Am I forgetting something?"

"Keegan said the two of you were having lunch today."

"I haven't even talked to Keegan since Friday before I picked Parker up. I thought he was going to be here since he was home for the weekend."

My parents shared a quick smile, and Mom shrugged. "You should call him then, he left about an hour ago."

Grabbing my phone from my back pocket, I pulled up Keegan's name, and tapped on it.

"Hey, sis."

"I thought you were going to be at Mom and Dad's today. I told Parker you would be here, he's been looking forward to seeing you."

"Aw, tell my little man I'll see him tonight. Now get your ass over here and have lunch with me."

I let out an exasperated groan. "I don't even know where *here* is, and why can't I just bring Parker with me?"

"I'm at Rio, and because we never have time to talk. So hurry up, I'm fucking starving."

Looking at my son playing with the toys that always stayed at my parents' house, I thought for a second and said, "Okay, but I'm bringing Parker."

"No, Ray. I want to see him, and I'll see him tonight. Just trust me on this, all right? Come alone."

Turning away from Parker, I hissed into the phone, "You're being sketchy and it's pissing me off."

"And you didn't come out on Friday, so we're even."

"Keegan—"

"Hurry up."

I growled into the phone when he hung up, and shoved it back in my pocket. My parents both waved at me from where they were pulling Parker into the kitchen. "Have fun, sweetheart!"

"Love you, Mom!" Parker called out.

"Are you all in on this?" I asked, looking at them suspiciously. "What is going on?"

My mom put her hands on her hips and shot me a look. "Oh, stop being so dramatic, Reagan. Go have lunch with your brother and give us some time with our grandson."

"Mom, it's summer, you have him five days a week!"

"Bye, honey!" She bent to whisper something, and Parker turned to look at me. "Bye, Mom!"

What the hell is going on? I stood there trying to think of something to say, but I was obviously outnumbered. With a defeated sigh, I waved and called out a good-bye before leaving the house and heading to Rio.

I was still grumbling to myself as I crossed the parking lot, when a deep voice from a few feet away had my body coming to a stop.

"So how about that name, huh?"

Turning slowly, my breath caught when I saw him standing there. Same cocky smirk, his tattoos on display beneath his black shirt, his dark eyes hidden from view behind aviators.

Biting down on the inside of my cheek so I wouldn't smile, I glanced around us before teasing him. "Are you following me now? It was just coffee and an old shirt."

He laughed and stepped closer. "I was about to ask you the same thing, but unfortunately for you, even though I've been thinking about you all weekend, I'm not stalking you. I'm meeting someone."

I didn't have to fight a smile anymore. *Is he serious?* "Ha. Wow. You're going to try and charm a girl out of her name when you're about to go on a date? Nice."

Not waiting for his response, I quickly walked into the restaurant, and my eyes narrowed on Keegan when I saw his girlfriend, Erica, with him. I loved her for my brother, but why hadn't Keegan said anything?

They both stood when they saw me, and after a hug from Erica, Keegan pulled me in for a bear hug.

"Good to see you, Ray."

"Why couldn't I bring Parker if Erica is here? Mom said it was just supposed to be us."

"Well . . ." His eyes glanced at something over my head, and a smile crossed his face as he released me.

Before I could turn around to see what he was smiling at, goose bumps covered my arms when *his* voice came from right behind me. "Still waiting on that name." I finally turned, and saw his black eyes were shooting daggers directly above my head. "And now I see why the two of you couldn't stop laughing on Friday."

"What?" I whispered. I was beyond confused, and still annoyed at this guy.

Erica gave the guy a tight hug before Keegan shrugged and slapped his shoulder. "You can't really be mad at me for this, can you?"

"Wait . . . what?" I asked again.

Keegan put a hand on my back, and held his other arm out toward the tattooed guy. "Reagan, this is my roommate I was telling you about, Coen Steele. Steele, this is my little sister, Reagan."

"You're Reagan?" Coen asked with a hint of amusement in his tone.

"You knew about this?" Anger and embarrassment quickly took over my confusion. I was going to punch them both in their throats.

"Uh, no. I thought Hudson owed me lunch for losing at pool the other night. Speaking of," he said suddenly as he looked back at my brother, "how did you know this was the girl?"

The girl? He'd told my brother about me?

"I was on the phone with Reagan when you ran into each other. I heard your voice, coulda sworn it was you . . . and then when you came into the bar that night, you confirmed it for us."

I still couldn't get past the fact that Coen had told my brother about me, and that this was the guy Keegan had tried to set me up with that same night.

"Come on." Keegan pushed me toward the table. "Let's sit down, everyone's starting to stare at us."

A tan, tattooed arm grabbed the back of my chair to pull it out, but stopped halfway. "I find it funny that you'd accuse *me* of flirting with you before a date . . . and apparently you and your brother had already been talking about me. You sure *you* didn't know about this?"

"If I would have known, I wouldn't have shown up," I gritted out, and then it hit me.

The way my parents had both been so eager to get me out of their house, and to watch Parker. The way Keegan had made sure I wouldn't bring my son. I felt betrayed by them suddenly. I'd told Keegan I didn't want to be set up with anyone, my mom and dad knew how I felt about this. And they'd all gone behind my back anyway.

Now all I wanted was to get my son and go home. To get away from all their opinions on my life. And to not. Fucking. Cry.

I schooled my expression and took two, deep breaths in and out, focusing on not tearing up when my eyes started burning. With a hard look directed at my brother, I turned and walked quickly away from them.

"Reagan!" Keegan's voice easily carried over the loud restaurant, but I didn't stop moving.

I was at my car, and had just thrown my purse into the passenger seat, when Keegan turned me and stopped me from getting in.

"What the hell, Ray?"

"How could you all do that to me?" I hissed at him, and locked my jaw to stop the quivering.

"We just—"

"Why can't you guys just be okay with the fact that I don't want to be with anyone? I don't *want* to date. I don't *want* to meet someone. I don't *need* a man in my—" I broke off with a sob, and slapped a hand over my mouth as tears filled my eyes.

At the sight of my tears, Keegan's face turned white. "Sis," he crooned as he reached for my cheek.

Slapping his hand away, I wiped quickly at my cheeks and pointed at him. "Don't fucking touch me! I expect for Mom to bring it up, but I would never think you *all* would go behind my back like *this*."

"Reagan, we just want you to—"

"I don't care what you all want!" I yelled, and started to get in my SUV. He tried to stop me, so I turned and shoved him away. "Fuck you, Keegan! You were supposed to be on *my* side."

I couldn't have moved him no matter how hard I tried, but he still took a step back and didn't try to stop me when I climbed in. He looked sick when I glanced at him one last time before pulling out of the parking space; and to my horror, Coen was standing outside the restaurant, his dark eyes focused on me. I don't know how long he'd been out there, or how much he'd heard. A part of me was mortified that he'd seen me break when I'd spent years making sure I never would again, but I knew I'd never see him again. So I swallowed my humiliation, and drove back to my parents' house.

Like with Keegan, my parents were so shocked to see me crying that neither had said anything or tried to stop me when I walked in, grabbed Parker, and walked back out with him.

The three of them endlessly called and texted me throughout the day, and twice Keegan had come over. But I never answered my phone, or the door. Was I overreacting? Was I being dramatic? Yeah, I probably was. But at the time, I didn't care. They'd gone behind my back on something they knew I was strongly against. They'd tried to put me in a situation I was too scared to put my son and myself in. So instead of talking to any of them, I spent the rest of the day playing with Parker and cuddling up on the couch to watch movies before he fell asleep. The entire time chanting to myself that we didn't need a man in our lives. That we were perfect just like this.

Coen—*August 20, 2010*

MY BODY FLEW up into a sitting position, and I struggled to fix my breathing. My hands were gripping the sheets as I fought against the tremors making their way through me. I was covered in a cold sweat, and even though I could see that I was in my condo, it took my mind another few seconds to catch up.

Memories. Nightmares. Night after night. Never

changing. Never giving me peace from what had happened.

Had, I told myself. *It's not happening right now. I'm in my bed. In my condo. In Colorado.*

Glancing at my phone, I sighed and let it fall onto the bed beside me. I'd stayed awake as long as I could last night and this morning editing photos, watching mindless TV, doing an impromptu shoot of myself at my studio, and then coming back to my place to edit those as well. I'd finally given in and crawled into my bed at eight this morning.

It was 9:45 A.M. now. Not even two hours of sleep, and already more than I could handle, apparently.

Flipping back the covers, I slowly got out of bed, and pulled off my sweat-soaked clothes as I walked to the bathroom. Turning the water on as hot as it could go, I waited until steam started filling the room before I got in . . . welcoming the burn as it hit my skin. Putting both hands against the wall, I dropped my head and let the hot water pour over my head and back as I waited.

The burning helped take my mind off the ingrained images that played over and over like a fucked-up video. Despite what Hudson said, I didn't need to talk to someone about what was going on. They wouldn't understand. Neither would Hudson.

Hudson, Saco, and I were all in the same unit, and though we didn't have your typical deployments, we had missions. Ones we weren't allowed to talk about with our families—not that we'd want to put them through that shit—and one that I couldn't talk about period. The only person that could understand that time to an extent was Saco. We'd been on a mission and had split up into four teams of five for one part . . . and it had all gone so fucking wrong. Saco and his team had found me; and he'd seen the destruction.

Out of respect for me, he hadn't told Hudson what he'd seen when he grabbed me. I respected the hell out of him for that since I knew they were both always worrying about me and trying to get me to get help. But they hadn't been there. Hadn't gone through it.

I waited until my mind was on nothing but the heat from the water before shutting it off and getting out of the shower. Pacing around my condo for a few minutes had my mind going back to places I couldn't have it go. So I pulled on mesh shorts, grabbed my running shoes, and walked out the door. I didn't care that I'd just been in the shower. It hadn't been to get clean; it had been to forget. And it hadn't been enough.

Taking off for the trail just off my backyard, I ran hard, trying to push all thoughts from my mind except for the pavement below me, and view around me.

I wasn't sure how long I'd been running when I came upon a park. Open area off to one side, a playground in the corner closest to me, and a lake on the far corner. And right in front of me, a blond standing off to the side of the playground. She was facing it, watching as she talked on her phone, her hand shielding her eyes from the sun. Hazel eyes that I'd been thinking of for five days since she'd stormed out of the restaurant.

Knowing I was probably the last person she wanted to see, and not having the best morning so far, I considered running in another direction so I wouldn't be tempted to talk to her. But she looked quickly over to me before doing a double take. Her mouth forming a perfect O as recognition settled over her face.

There was no way I wasn't stopping now.

Slowing down as I approached her, I noticed her eyes kept darting between me and the kids using the playground, and I wondered which one was her son.

"Reagan," I said, and tried to catch my breath.

She didn't respond, but I could hear a woman ask through her phone, "Who's that?"

Reagan floundered for a second, and I almost told her my name, but I didn't want to let on that I could hear her friend. "Um, uh, it's Keegan's friend from the army. The one from the coffee sh—"

She hadn't gotten the rest of the word out when the other voice said excitedly, "The hot Asian?"

I couldn't help it, I burst out laughing and had to turn away from her for a second when I saw her cheeks stain red.

"I, uh, I have to go." She quickly tapped on her phone and shoved it in her back pocket before running her hands over her cheeks.

I wanted to tell her they were as red as she feared, but knew she was embarrassed enough.

"Uh . . . hi, Coen."

"So you do know my name?" I asked, teasing her.

"Why are you here?"

I looked around, and back on the trail I'd come from. "This trail goes right past my backyard. Why are you here? Shouldn't you be at work or something?"

Her eyes darted back to the playground, and she licked her lips like she was nervous. "My uh—my office shuts down every first and third Friday of the month."

"Sounds like an awesome job."

"Perks of working for a local company, I guess." Her eyes went back to the playground for a second. "I should probably go."

Not looking away from her, I nodded my head in the direction of the play equipment. "Which one is your son?"

Reagan's entire body froze, and the hand that had been brushing back her long hair stopped mid-action. "Who told you I have a son?" her voice was now careful and defensive.

"Your brother. Look, I'm sorry, I didn't mean to scare you."

"Keegan," she grumbled, but her body relaxed. "It's fine, I just didn't know you knew. I should have figured since you used to be roommates . . . I just—I don't—"

"You don't let a lot of people into your son's life, I know. I don't blame you."

Her eyes had hardened at first, but widened with

my last statement. "I don't know whether to be pissed that you know all this about me, or curious as to why you don't blame me."

Grabbing the shirt from where it'd been hanging at my side, I ran it over my face and chest, and noticed her eyes followed the path. They lingered on the tattoos on my chest before slowly drifting over my arms. But her face gave nothing away; for all I knew, they could disgust her.

"In all fairness to your brother," I started, and her eyes snapped back up to mine, "he didn't tell me anything about you or your son until the day I got out. All I'd known was he was always going back home to be with the two of you. I finally asked him."

"And what all did he tell you?" The defensive tone was back, and I fought a smile. Reagan was cute when she got all protective.

"Not much, but enough for me to admire you and your strength."

From the way her head jerked slightly back and her eyelids blinked rapidly, she hadn't been expecting that answer. After watching me for a few seconds, she crossed her arms over her chest, and leveled me with a glare. "Did Keegan set you up to this? Did he tell you I'd be here today? Because as I'm sure you heard last weekend, I'm not interested in . . . well, anything."

"Look, I know you were burned, so you're cautious now; but not everyone has a hidden agenda."

"I've never seen you before in my life, and then I see you three times within a week? Keegan tried to get me to come out and have a beer with you. He *admitted* he was trying to set me up with you. Then out of nowhere, you're right behind me in Starbucks, I see you two days later at lunch, and not even a week later you're at the park that I spend a lot of Fridays at with Parker? Excuse me for not believing you."

"Wow, really?" I laughed and rubbed at my jaw. "Okay, yeah, I get it. But I'd also been in the army for the last six years and had just gotten out when I ran into you. I have a studio not even five minutes from that Starbucks and have been going there for years. Your brother is one of my best friends, and he owed me lunch for losing a game, as I told you. I just woke up and decided to run on the same path I've been using every day since I moved into my place early this week, and this is where it led me. Granted, I hadn't been this far yet, but I can assure you, Duchess, I didn't come this far for you. I haven't talked to Hudson in a couple days . . . and before your crazy mind starts coming up with other shit, I don't know where the fuck you live."

Her hazel eyes narrowed and she took a step closer. "Did I *ask* if you knew?"

"You sure as shit were getting there with all the other bullshit you're accusing me of."

"Do you realize you're standing on a playground, surrounded by little kids, and you keep cussing?"

"Do you realize your holier-than-thou attitude to hide what you're really thinking and feeling makes you look like a bitch?"

Her eyebrows shot up, and her mouth opened with a soft huff.

"I know you're careful, I told you, I get it. But nothing during the times I've seen you has made you come across as someone who's independent and wanting to keep her life private. With the shit you're spouting off, swear to God I would think you're the most vain person I've ever met if I didn't know any better. The world doesn't revolve around you, and people don't make it their mission in life to make *yours* a living hell."

"I never said they did," she gritted out.

"Really? I complimented you, and you immediately took it as something your brother must have set up. Because, heaven forbid, someone compliments you, and actually means it."

"After everything else you just said about me, do you really think I would trust any compliment from you?"

Closing the distance between us, I bent my head so I was whispering in her ear. "That's exactly my point. I compliment you, and you think it's bullshit. I tell you that this mask you're wearing makes you come off as someone I'm sure you're not, and say that if I didn't know any better, I would *think* you're vain; and you automatically come to the conclusion that's what I really think about you. You hear what you want to hear because it helps you keep up your guard."

"You're such an asshole."

"Who's cussing now?" Her hand came up to my

bare chest, but instead of putting pressure against it, her fingers subtly curled against my skin. I moved so I could see her face, and had to bite back a smile when I noticed her eyes were zeroed in on her hand and my chest. Her breathing got heavier, and each breath brought us closer together again. "Drop the front, Reagan. The tough, uncaring act isn't flattering. I don't know you, but from the few glimpses I've seen when you've dropped your guard, and what I've heard, this isn't you. You're protecting yourself and you don't trust guys—understandably—but we're not all bad."

"Coming from the guy who said I act like a bitch," she said, and looked up at me. Her face would have been unreadable if it weren't for her eyes, which were bright with amusement.

"I was proving a point, and you *were* acting like a bitch. Sorry if you don't like honesty, but if you give me shit, be prepared to get it right back."

"You're a real charmer, you know that? And why do you say that like we'll see each other again? After this lovely encounter, I'm pretty sure I'll be avoiding you and your arrogant mouth at all costs."

"There you go acting like you don't care again. Don't forget . . . I *did* hear your friend refer to me as 'the hot Asian.' "

Her cheeks went red again, and just as she opened her mouth to respond, a small voice came from beside us.

"Mom . . . ?"

Reagan quickly pushed away from me, and we

both turned to see two boys standing there. One with blond hair just like his mom's.

"Hey, honey, what's up?" Reagan asked, her voice shaky.

He looked over at me before looking back at his mom. "Who's he?"

She had a lost look on her face when she glanced at me, and I just raised an eyebrow waiting for her response. "He's uh . . . he's Uncle Keegan's friend. His name's Coen."

His chest puffed out as he crossed his arms and glared up at me. I had no doubt he'd perfected that look by watching his mom. "Are you being mean to my mom?"

I couldn't help it, I barked out a laugh and bent down so I was eye level with him. "No way, bud. Because I'd be too scared of you coming to kick my butt if I were."

"Oh God," Reagan muttered, and I wondered if "butt" was a bad word for a kid his age.

He watched me for a few more seconds, like he was trying to figure out if he should still try to save his mom from me, before he relaxed his stance and pointed at the arm that was fully sleeved. "I like your arms. The stars are cool," he said, and tapped one of three stars on my forearm.

"Yeah? Well maybe we'll have to get you one."

"Really?" he asked excitedly at the same time Reagan groaned. "Are you kidding?"

I stood and looked at her. "What? It would wash off after a few days."

"Seriously, Coen?" She rolled her eyes at me and shook her head.

"Do yours wash off too?"

Looking back at the boys, I bent down again to talk to them. "No, but that's 'cause I'm older."

"How old until mine won't wash off?"

"Never," Reagan said at the same time I shrugged and said, "At least eighteen. So what, you have about two . . . three years left until then?"

Parker and his friend laughed. "I'm only six!"

"Six? Really? Hmm." I clicked my tongue and made a face. "Guess you'll have to hold off for a while then, yeah?"

"Oh my God, this isn't happening," Reagan huffed.

I shot her a wink as I stood back up. She returned it with a glare.

"Parker, what'd you come over here for? Are you ready to go home?"

"Oh! Mom, can I stay at Jason's tonight? He already asked his mom and she said I could, so can I? Please, Mom?"

If I hadn't been watching her, I wouldn't have seen the look of panic that crossed her face before she could cover it with a smile. "Wow, um, you sure you want to?"

"Yes, Mom, please!"

"Well, let me go talk to Jason's mom, and I'll let you know, okay? Go play."

Parker seemed to take that as a "yes" because he high-fived his friend before running back to the jungle gym.

Looking back at Reagan, I noticed the panic was back in her eyes and walked closer to her. "First sleepover?"

Her head turned quickly to face me, and her hands went to play with the ends of her hair. "He's only ever stayed at my parents' house before."

"Does he know the Jason kid well?"

"Yeah, they were in the same class last year, he's his best friend. I've only met his mom a few times, but she's really nice."

"I'm sure he'll be fine, and if he's not, he'll call you and you can pick him up."

"It's not Parker I'm worried about, it's—wait, why am I even discussing this with you? For some reason I doubt you have kids, which means you have no idea what this is like. And you've only known my son and me for five minutes, you don't have a say in any of this."

Touching her arm, I turned her so we were facing each other and closed the distance between us. Her breathing started picking up pace again, and I waited for her to drag her eyes from my chest until she was looking up at me. "No, I don't have kids. I just remember what it was like being that age. And I know I don't have any say, and I'm not trying to. But anyone could have seen how close you were to freaking out, so I was trying to help you by getting you to talk about it instead of keeping everything inside."

"I really hate how you act like you know me."

"Never said I did, but you're not hard to read, Reagan." Leaning closer, I stared at her hazel eyes and whispered, "I also never said I didn't *want* to know you."

She inhaled softly, and neither of us moved as we continued staring at each other. Our faces were close enough that I could smell the mint from her gum, and I had to lock my body so I wouldn't pull her closer so I could see if her lips were as soft as they looked. *This is bad. She's Hudson's sister.* She also had over six years' worth of baggage that came in the form of not trusting any man.

Swallowing hard, I looked away and said, "You should probably go talk to Jason's mom."

When I glanced back at her, she was blinking slowly, like coming out of a daze. *Then again . . . she also said Hudson had been trying to set us up . . .* She didn't say anything as she turned away, so I pulled her back.

"If you do let him go, and you don't want to be alone tonight, your brother will know how to get ahold of me."

"Don't wait around for that to happen." I couldn't hold back my smile at the way her voice came out all breathy.

"I'll see you tonight, Reagan," I assured her as I took a few steps back.

"I said *don't*."

"I know what you said. Have a good rest of your day." With a wink, I turned and started the run back to my condo.

She didn't make any more protests, and I didn't stop smiling the entire way home. From what I'd seen of her, I wouldn't put it past her to ignore me just to spite me. But I'd also seen her reaction to me, and because of that, I spent the rest of the day doing nothing but thinking of her, and waiting for a call.

Chapter Three

Reagan—*August 20, 2010*

I PACED AROUND my apartment for thirty minutes after I'd dropped Parker off. It wasn't my first night without him, but it was the first he'd be with someone other than my parents. And even those nights were rare. I was seriously considering going back to pick him up, but he'd been so excited to go . . . I couldn't do that to him.

I so did not want Parker growing up having me as his only friend. Those mom-and-son pairs who were so close the guy ended up not dating when he got older because he was such a momma's boy were creepy, and I didn't want that for my son. I loved having our nights alone at home, but I wanted him to have a fun life, I wanted him to have friends like Jason, and girlfriends later . . . way later. I just hadn't realized he was old enough for this stage yet.

Sitting on the couch, I turned on the TV and stared at it, not paying attention to what was on, as my legs continued to bounce up and down. Glancing at the clock, I groaned when I saw it was only five. This was going to be the longest night ever.

My eyes kept darting to my phone sitting on the coffee table, and I tried to think of someone to call. Anyone. Well, anyone other than Coen.

I didn't need to call Keegan to get Coen's number; Keegan had sent it to me early this week. His text had said it was in case of an emergency, but I wasn't dumb, I knew why he'd sent it to me. I just hadn't considered using it.

Until now.

Standing quickly, I walked into my kitchen and stared into the pantry, and then the fridge, looking for something to make for dinner. But I wasn't seeing anything. I was freaking the fuck out because my son was having his first sleepover! Slamming the refrigerator door shut, I went back to pacing around my living room for another few minutes as I nervously played with the ends of my long hair.

I considered calling my mom for about five seconds before I realized how ridiculous that was. I'm twenty-two. I have a free night for the first time in a long time, and I want to call my mom? When did I turn into an old lady?

Walking to the coffee table, I bent and grabbed at my phone, determined to call one of my friends. But instead I was opening up Keegan's texts and scrolling up until I reached the number. Before I could talk myself out of it, I pressed the number and hit CALL.

"Hello?"

"Distract me," I blurted out.

There were a few seconds of silence, before his deep voice asked, "Duchess?"

Goose bumps covered my body, and I swear to God I had to stop myself from whimpering. This morning replayed through my head, the way his lean, muscled body had been covered in a fine sheen of sweat. The way his chest had felt under my hand. His tattoos.

I hated tattoos. Hated them. But I'd wanted to trace every one of his. I'd wanted to study every picture and word covering his arms and chest. I'd wanted to see what the letters on his fingers spelled out. I'd wanted to watch his tattooed hands as they touched me.

Bad. Bad. So bad. Calling him was the wrong thing to do.

Clearing my throat, I tried to put force behind my words, but I failed miserably. "I'll hang up if you call me that again."

He laughed softly. "Reagan."

"Yes?"

Another laugh and I had to sit down on the couch when my legs started shaking. "You're the one who called me. Shouldn't I be asking you that?"

"Oh, um. I need you to distract me."

"Parker go to his friend's house?"

I made some sort of affirmative noise, worried that if I said it out loud, I'd start freaking out all over again.

"Do you want me to come pick you up?"

"No!" I shouted, and scrambled to find something to say. "I—I just—can I just come over?"

I didn't want him in my apartment. This was my place with Parker, and having Coen here didn't seem right. If he came over, if he got comfortable being here, that would be a step in the direction of letting him into Parker's life as well. I didn't care that he'd met Parker . . . I was already over what had happened this morning; but I wasn't ready for him to be here yet. And if we went out and happened to run into my parents or their friends, I would never hear the end of it. My mom would start planning a wedding the second she knew his name. Or maybe when she got over me actually bringing someone into Parker's life.

"Sure . . . ?"

"I'm sorry, I just don't want to go out."

"Okay," he said carefully. "Well, yeah, you're more than welcome to come here. Have you eaten?"

"No."

"All right, we'll order something when you get here."

I stood there playing with the ends of my hair for a few seconds before I said, "This isn't a date."

"Of course not," he said, his tone amused. "It's a distraction."

"Right." A very, very bad distraction.

He gave me his address before we hung up, and I ran into my closet. A part of me told me to go in my yoga pants and shirt, since that's what he'd seen me in earlier and I didn't want him to think I'd dressed for him. But another wanted to look like more than a tired mom when I was around him.

After going through three outfits, I settled on a pair of short black shorts and a light gray off-the-shoulder shirt. Casual, and comfy . . . and hopefully I didn't look like I had tried as hard as I did to look both. With a quick touch-up to my makeup, I grabbed my phone, purse, and keys and left my apartment before I could talk myself into staying there instead.

During the ten-minute drive there, I tried to make myself turn around the entire time. Even as I walked up to his condo, I kept chanting to myself how bad of an idea this was, and how I needed to go back home. When he answered the door in low-slung jeans and another black shirt, I almost turned around and walked away.

Such a bad idea.

"You look beautiful." His dark eyes slowly raked over my body before resting on my face again.

"This isn't a date," I reminded him again, and he laughed.

"And you still can't take a compliment." Opening the door wider, he stepped back to give me room. "Come in, I'm starving."

I stood there for a few seconds before barely turning back toward his driveway. "Maybe I should—"

Coen grabbed my hand and pulled me into his condo before shutting the door behind us. "Stop second-guessing everything. You wanted a distrac-

tion, and I'm hungry. So we're going to have our it's-
not-a-date-it's-a-distraction night, and you're going to
learn how to relax."

"I know how to relax."

"You sure about that?" he asked, the rise of one
eyebrow challenging me to argue.

I couldn't.

HOURS LATER, WE were full on pizza, and had been
watching movies on Coen's TV. I'd laughed more tonight that I usually did in a week's time, and as the
hours had passed, I'd slowly felt myself relaxing into
him. Something about his easygoing laugh, his no-
bullshit attitude, and mesmerizing eyes had left me
leaning into him more, and enjoying his company . . .
and being terrified of that.

"I shit you not"—he pointed at the screen and
leaned forward so he could look at me—"that's Casey
from *Teenage Mutant Ninja Turtles*."

I laughed and grabbed the remote to rewind *Shutter
Island* before pausing on the man in question. "That?
No, that is *not* Casey. I would know because I thought
he was so hot in that movie."

Coen looked over at me with a look of disgust.
"That's gross. He's old. Obviously," he said, pointing
at the TV.

"That's not him! I'm telling you."

"No, what you're telling me is you go for guys who
are thirty years older than you. Gold digger."

I laughed harder and reached for my phone on the table.

"What are you doing?"

"I'm looking it up, I'm going to prove you wrong!"

Coen grabbed my phone from me and held it out of my reach.

"Give it back! Or are you worried you're going to be wrong?"

"No. Fuck no. I know that's him, I'm just thinking about you and your reaction when you realize that *Teenage Mutant Ninja Turtles* was made twenty years ago."

I stopped reaching and cocked my head to the side. "Seriously?"

"Yeah, Duchess."

My eyes narrowed on him. "I hate that name."

"And you wonder why I keep calling you it."

"Asshole," I growled as I reached over to make another grab for my phone.

His arm kept it just out of reach, so I rolled to my knees and leaned over him, stretching my arm as he stretched his body away from me. One of his hands had gone to my waist to keep me from moving, but the air around us seemed to change at the same time his fingers flexed against me.

Forgetting my phone, I looked down at Coen to see him staring at me. His face no longer looked amused, he almost looked mad. But that look had my body heating, and my breaths getting heavy.

"Reagan"—he cleared his throat—"I need you to

get off me before I do something you're not going to like."

Lean back. Lean back. Get off him. I didn't move, I stayed right there, staring at his dark eyes before mine involuntarily dropped to his mouth.

"Reagan," he said in warning.

Lean back. For the love of God, lean back. "How do you know I won't like it?" I found myself asking, and before I had time to try to take it back, Coen let my phone fall to the ground and grabbed the back of my neck to bring my face down to his.

Coen's lips captured mine on a growl, and my body shivered against him as I let myself rest on his chest. His tongue prompted my lips to part, and I gripped at his shirt when he started teasing me with slow strokes of his tongue, and soft bites against my bottom lip.

Without ever letting his lips leave mine, he pushed me back until our positions were switched. My back to the couch, with him on top of me. His lips moved to my neck, and I rolled my head back, giving him more access. I didn't want a man in my life, and had been fine without one ever since Austin. But since I'd run into him a week ago, something about Coen and his dark eyes had left me craving him. A craving I'd tried to ignore. But now, with some of his body weight pressing me into the couch, one hand in my hair, and the other keeping himself somewhat propped up; I not only couldn't ignore it, I didn't want him to ever stop touching me.

I knew this was dangerous ground. I knew he had

the potential of shattering me. I knew this was going too fast . . . but I wanted more. My hands trailed down his chest, and when they kept going down, he pushed himself up to give me room. Grabbing the bottom of his shirt, I slowly pulled it up until he sat back on his knees and took it the rest of the way off before lowering himself again.

The muscles in his stomach contracted when I ran my hands back up to his chest, over his shoulders and down his tattooed arms. Turning my head, I pressed a kiss to his arm, before moving to his chest and kissing the words there. He tugged on my hair so my head would fall back again, and just before his lips touched mine, my phone started ringing.

"Ignore it," I whispered, and captured his mouth.

His hand left my hair, and trailed down my upper body, his fingers barely grazing the swell of my breast as he did. As soon as his hand started running back up, now on my bare skin, my phone rang again. I arched my back when his fingers touched the lace of my bra . . . and then it hit me.

"Parker!" I shouted, and started to push Coen away, but he was already off the couch and grabbing my phone to hand to me. "Hello?" I said breathlessly into the phone.

"Mommy?"

My heart broke when I recognized his sobs. "Oh God, what's wrong?"

"Can you come get me?"

"Of course I can, baby. Are you okay?"

"Yeah—I just—can I come home?"

I righted my shirt and started to stand, but Coen pushed me back onto the couch. I shot him a look, but his expression was calm and understanding, and a sense of peace washed over me at I looked into his dark eyes.

"Of course," I repeated into the phone. "Let me talk to Jason's mom, okay?"

The sound of the phone being shuffled between hands filled the other end of the line before I heard, "Hey, Reagan, he's fine. He just woke up crying and said he wanted to go home. I'm so sorry, they had so much fun tonight, it must just be because this is so different."

I sighed in relief that nothing had happened to him. "No, no, don't be sorry. It's more than fine, I'm on my way right now. Thank you for calling me." When we hung up, I looked back into Coen's eyes. "Could you hear?"

He nodded. "Yeah, I'm sorry for stopping you, but I couldn't let you run out of here when you were on the edge of freaking out."

"I know, and I appreciate it." My eyes moved over his face for a few seconds before I stood. "I have to go."

Coen stood and walked me to the door, and when I turned to say good-bye, I saw the concern in his eyes. He was afraid I would regret what had just been happening. Grabbing the handle of the door, he opened it and stepped back, his eyes never leaving mine. "Drive safe, it's late and—just drive safe."

I wanted to regret it. I wanted to tell him I couldn't see him again. Having Parker call while I'd been kissing Coen made me want to keep him from Parker's life and mine all over again.

Want to. That didn't mean I could.

Bringing one hand around his neck, I stood on my toes and softly pressed my lips to his. The arm not holding the door wrapped around my waist to pull me closer as he deepened the kiss for a few seconds before releasing me.

"Good night," I whispered against his lips, and kissed him one last time when they curled up in a smile.

"Night."

I walked quickly to my car, and thanked God that Coen lived closer to Jason's than I did.

After picking up my still-crying son, I drove us home and got him into his own bed once he'd calmed down. When I was sure he was asleep, I closed his door behind me and went to make sure the apartment was locked up, and all the lights were shut off.

Grabbing my phone after I got ready to go to sleep and had climbed into my bed, I pulled up Coen's name.

We made it home . . . you know . . . even though it's late and all ;)

Instead of a response, his name popped up on my screen, and I hit the green button.

"Hello," I answered quietly.

"I'm glad you made it back."

A smile crossed my face and I grabbed at the ends of my hair. "Sorry we had to cut the night short."

He was silent for a few seconds before saying, "Just tell me that won't be the last time I see you."

"As long as it's not a date," I teased.

"Never. I was thinking more of a distraction."

"I like distractions."

"So do I." His gruff tone had my eyes shutting and a shiver running down my body. "Get some sleep."

"You too."

"Good night, Reagan."

I hung up, and placed my phone on the nightstand. Just as I got comfortable in my bed, my phone vibrated.

Pulling up the text from Coen, I laughed out loud when I saw the three images. One was a screenshot of the cast of *Teenage Mutant Ninja Turtles*; right in the center was the man who played Casey. The second was of him now. The third was a list of his movies, and right there was the title *Shutter Island*.

I'm going to act like I never saw that. He's still Casey in my head.

Coen Steele: Denial is a bitch.

Putting my phone back on the nightstand. I closed my eyes and went to sleep with a smile on my face.

Chapter Four

Coen—*August 25, 2010*

"Chin down just a little bit more. Eyes right at me. Mouth a little softer . . . perf—"

"Damn, Steele!"

I straightened from the position I'd been in and turned, my mouth already curving up in a smile.

"If this is what you do all day, no wonder you wanted to get out so bad."

Slapping Hudson's hand when he approached me, I just shrugged. "Well, seeing how it's a Wednesday night and you're not on base . . . I can only guess that means one of two things."

He held his hands out to the side and smirked. "Civilian status, bitch!"

"Really, man? Congrats. Let's go grab a drink when I'm done, we only have a few more minutes."

Hudson flopped down into a chair and grinned. "Don't let me stop you."

I rolled my eyes and turned back to my client. She was already only covered by her underwear and an unbuttoned shirt, but now with Hudson sitting next to me, her eyes were glued to him and she was pulling her unbuttoned shirt wider.

"Eyes back on me," I said for the third time since he'd come in. "Stop biting on your lip. Stop eye-fucking Hudson. He's taken."

Standing, I glared over at Hudson and kicked his leg as I pointed to the door. "Get the fuck out."

"Hater," he mumbled as he stood and left the studio.

Looking back at my client, I raised an eyebrow at her. It wasn't my place to remind her she was doing this shoot for her husband. "All right, you ready for the ones on the couch?"

After we were done with the shoot and she was fully dressed again, I yelled out for Hudson as I flipped through the pictures I'd gotten.

"We got a ton of great shots," I told her as I continued to look through my camera. "I'll work on these and send you the best in a few days, all right?"

"Perfect! Thank you so much for this, I hope he likes them." She straightened up when Hudson came closer to us, and I stopped going through the pictures to watch them.

"Taken." I reminded her when she gave Hudson a look I knew Erica would kill her for.

"Right. Well, you both have a good night."

As soon as she was gone, I pointed at the door and glared at Hudson. "Married."

"Eh." He made a face like that fact had just made her lose all appeal.

"Exactly."

"It's not my fault they want this." He said seriously and waved a hand down his body before busting up laughing.

"I don't know how Erica puts up with you." I turned and put my camera away before going to turn everything off.

"You know I wouldn't do anything."

"Yeah, and you and I both know she wants to chop your dick off every time you look at another girl. I fear for your life the day she sees you hitting on another chick."

He sighed. "I don't hit on them. Did you hear me trying to pick up on that girl at all? No. And she was asking for it. They want to look at me, I'm not going to stop them."

I snorted. "All right. If that's how you see it. Just ask Erica to give me time to get there to save your sorry ass before she decides to kill you one of these days. Come on, let's go grab a beer."

"Uh, actually . . . meeting up with my family at a restaurant tonight, but I stopped by because I wanted you to come. We haven't talked much since you got out, and I figured after dinner we could chill and catch up."

"Your family?" I stopped walking.

"Yeah. Knowing you, I bet you don't leave your studio or condo except to get from one to the other. You're probably eating nothing but ramen noodles. You probably only talk to the people whose photos you're taking. And I just know you're not sleeping. So I want you to come have actual food. Talk to people about other things . . . you know, normal night out."

"Uh . . ." I still hadn't moved from my spot. It'd been five days since Reagan came to my apartment. We'd talked every day, but I hadn't seen her again since. "Is your sister going to be there?"

"Obviously." Hudson shot me a weird look before understanding crossed over his face. "Swear to God, she won't freak out on you or me this time. I'll have you two sit at opposite ends of the table if it'll be better."

Which means she hadn't told Hudson. Or her parents probably. And I wasn't about to tell Hudson that his little sister had spent most of last Friday night in my apartment. Which made this even more awkward. "Yeah, maybe I shouldn't go."

"No, dude, I want you there. Erica hasn't seen you in a couple weeks either and she'll be there. Come on."

With a defeated sigh, I shook my head and started walking out of my studio again. "All right. Let's go."

Reagan—*August 25, 2010*

I PULLED BACK from hugging Erica and looked behind her, my eyebrows pinching together in confusion. "Is Keegan not with you?"

"No, he came in a couple hours ago to hang out at his friend's studio before dinner. So he's meeting us here."

My eyes widened, and I was glad Erica had turned to hug my mom so she wouldn't notice my expression. I didn't doubt she'd left Coen's name out because of the way I'd reacted at lunch a couple weeks ago, and there was no way she could've known that I knew about Coen's studio. Because she didn't know about us hanging out.

No one did.

Keegan wouldn't bring Coen with him, would he?

Of all the days for Parker to lose my phone in the apartment while it was on silent . . . why today?

"Mom, you okay?"

I looked down at Parker and plastered a smile on my face. "Of course I am. Why?"

He studied me for a second. I swear . . . six going on twenty. "You look scared."

"I'm not scared, honey. Are you excited to see—"

"Uncle Keegan!" he shouted, and darted past me.

He won't be here. He won't be here.

"Duchess."

Fuck, he's here.

I turned and couldn't figure out if I wanted to step away from him so no one would notice how badly I was craving him, or if I wanted to close the distance between us so I could feel the man whose warm voice had been the last thing to fill my world before I'd fallen asleep the last five nights.

"Have you not been getting my texts?" he asked hesitantly. "I tried warning you that I was coming."

"Parker lost my phone in the apartment."

I was losing the fight in staying away from him. My body was slowly inching closer to him, and it physically ached to keep my arms at my side instead of wrapping them around his waist.

How had this happened? Friday had been . . . well, it hadn't been what I'd expected it to be when I'd gone over there. I hadn't been expecting our kisses. I hadn't been expecting to get so lost in him that I wouldn't want to leave. But what I really hadn't expected was for this arrogant man to somehow creep his way into my life to the point where I woke up excited for my morning texts from him. Or how I couldn't wait for Parker to go to sleep at night because I knew I'd get to talk to Coen until I fell asleep.

"I know your brother doesn't know . . . do your parents?"

"No," I mouthed, and hated the flash of disappointment in his eyes.

"Hey!"

Coen and I moved away from each other and looked down at Parker.

"You're the guy from the park with the cool arms!"

Coen's face easily morphed into a smile as he held up his hand for Parker to slap. I was still as stone as everyone in my family and Erica eyed me curiously.

"How're you doing, bud?" Coen asked, and bent down so he was closer to Parker's height.

"Good. I'm still not old enough, you know." He tapped Coen's arm. "Mine would still wash off."

Coen laughed and nodded before glancing at me. "Yeah, you've got a while for that one."

I tried to smile at them. But my parents and Erica were still watching me. Keegan was now watching Coen and Parker. All of them looked confused.

"What's your name?"

"Coen."

Parker nodded. "That's right. Because you're Uncle Keegan's friend." Coen started responding when Parker added, "But you're Mom's friend too because you come see her at the park."

Oh. Jesus. Christ.

Coen looked up at me with a questioning look that was borderline challenging. I just stared back at him, not knowing what to say or what to do since everyone was still watching both of us.

Looking back at Parker, Coen smiled. "Yeah, bud, you could say that."

Erica looked confused, Keegan was glaring at Coen, Dad was now sizing up Coen, and Mom was staring at me with eyebrows practically up to her hairline.

"Your table is ready, if you all want to follow me this way!"

It took a few seconds for any of us to move, and even then, it was Parker who broke the spell we all seemed to be under. "Coen, sit next to me!"

Turning to follow him, I hadn't walked two steps before Coen walked past me and whispered in my ear, "That is, unless his mom is embarrassed for her family to know about me."

"Coen," I protested, but didn't say anything else as he caught up to Parker and the seating hostess.

"Am I missing something?" Keegan asked as we walked toward the table.

"Uh . . ."

"Because the last time the two of you saw each other, you got really pissed off and stormed out of the restaurant. Right?"

"Not exactly." I don't know why I felt like I was going to die. Keegan had tried setting us up, for shit's sake, he'd given me Coen's number!

"What do you mean not exactly?"

"I just mean not exactly. Why do you care?" I demanded, and began rounding the table to sit on the opposite side of Parker from Coen when Keegan caught my arm and spoke close to my ear.

"I just meant for you to go on *one* date with the guy so you would realize what you were missing in your life, Ray. I didn't mean for something to actually start between the two of you. And neither of you told me."

Looking over at Coen talking to Parker, I shrugged. "There's not much to tell yet."

"Really? Parker knows him and there's not much to tell?"

"You know you're really frustrating, Keegan," I hissed, and faced him. "You want me to date, but you don't. You want Parker to have a dad, but you don't like that Coen met him *accidentally* when Parker and I were at the park and Coen was running the trail that goes through there."

"Okay, you two," Mom said, pushing us apart. "You have people staring at you, and, Keegan, your friend can only keep Parker entertained for so long before Parker realizes that you and his mom are fighting. So let's just sit down and enjoy tonight. I don't want to start the first night of you being out of the army with the two of you fighting."

Keegan released my arm and pulled out a chair for Erica, and I walked past Coen and Parker to sit down. Coen gave me a confused look before continuing his conversation with Parker, and I tried to ignore the stares of my family as I stared blankly at the menu.

Even though this was supposed to be a dinner for Keegan, it quickly turned into an interrogation dinner. Even though Keegan and Coen were best friends, it was like Keegan was seeing Coen in a whole new light now that he was worried we were dating, and kept staring at him like he was trying to figure out a ridiculously hard math equation. Once Erica stopped looking confused, she couldn't keep her eyes off Coen and Parker as they joked and drew on Parker's menu together—a smile tugging at her lips the entire time. My dad had sat there with his arms crossed over his chest until Coen and Keegan's talks of their time in the army had Dad softening up and throwing in his own stories of his time in the navy. And Mom . . . dear God, I wanted to die for Coen, with the horrified look she was giving him for the first thirty minutes. Her eyes kept going back and forth between the small gauges in his ears and his arms covered in tattoos; each time they'd make a new trip, she looked like she was more disturbed by them. But once Coen started talking about his photography business, she was sucked in too.

"Parker, keep eating," I requested softly when he ate only two bites and pushed his plate back to continue coloring.

" 'Kay," he muttered distractedly, but never made a move toward his plate again.

"Par—"

"That all you gonna eat, bud?" Coen rested his head on his folded arms and nudged Parker with his shoulder. Before Parker could respond, Coen nodded in the direction of Keegan. "Don't you want to grow up all big and strong like your uncle?"

Parker stopped coloring and looked at Keegan before looking at Coen. "Are you not strong?"

"Me?" Coen's eyebrows raised and he shook his head. "Nah, I'm pretty weak." He sighed. "It's because I didn't eat my food growing up," he whispered loudly.

"No, you're not!" Parker laughed and pushed on his arm, and Coen dramatically moved away.

"I am, look." He placed his elbow on the table with his hand up for Parker to grab. "See if you can beat me in arm wrestling." Parker just continued to laugh as he set himself up. "Now don't think I'll go easy on you because you're only six."

"One-two-three, go!" Parker said quickly, and slammed Coen's hand down on the table. "You didn't try!"

"I did! I told you, I'm not strong. Come on, we'll go again."

I watched as they set up again, and covered my massive smile with my hand as I watched Coen give the slightest pressure before letting Parker beat him.

"Now see if you can beat your uncle."

Parker turned and looked at Keegan, his face lit up like I'd never seen it before. "Come on, Uncle Keegan! I bet I can beat you!"

Keegan's eyes flashed over to Coen's before meeting mine. His face was devoid of emotion, but the smile was clear in his eyes. "All right, little man. Let's do this."

Keegan beat Parker three times before Coen leaned close to Parker again. "See? Your uncle is really strong. Do you want to grow up to be like him, or weak like me?"

"Strong like Uncle Keegan."

Coen nodded toward Parker's plate. "Then you better eat up, bud."

Parker grinned widely at him as he pulled his plate closer to him and took a huge bite out of his burger.

It was in that moment that the attraction and excitement of everything that was Coen changed for me. It was then that I started falling for him. And though that terrified me, I knew I wouldn't try to stop myself from this.

"REAGAN, WHY DON'T you let Parker come stay with us tonight?" Mom offered as we all exited the restaurant.

"Wait, what? Why?"

She gave me a look before letting her eyes drift to Coen for a second. "Because your brother is finally home, and his girlfriend is here in town with him. The four of you should hang out."

"Four. Really, Mom?" I said so low no one else could hear us.

"Yeah, go do . . . whatever it is you all do now. And we'll just take him for the night so you won't have to worry about waking him up whenever you guys are done hanging out."

I stared at my mom with wide eyes before finally giving in. I wanted to spend time with Coen, and despite dinner just now . . . I still wasn't ready for the three of us to hang out together. So nights when Parker was with my parents were the only time I would be able to see him.

"Um, okay . . . but I don't have a bag for him or anything."

Mom waved me off and held her hand out for Parker. "We'll be fine."

Turning, I found Coen watching me thoughtfully and had to swallow a few times before asking, "Is it—uh, is it okay if I crash your night?"

Coen's dark gaze flitted over to my parents before resting back on my face. "Of course it is. We can all go to my place and chill. I just need Hudson to take me back to my studio to get my car," he said as he turned to look at my brother, and Keegan nodded as he continued talking to Erica about driving arrangements.

"Can I take you? I mean—I can take you," I blurted out before I could talk myself out of it.

"All right then," he said after a few seconds, and said good-bye to my parents as I said good night to Parker.

"Wasn't expecting that," Coen said as he put the address in my GPS when we were in my car.

"What?"

"For you to ask if you could drive me in front of your parents. From what I was gathering, you weren't exactly happy that they thought we'd hung out at the park. God forbid they know about Friday night."

"Coen—"

"You should probably start driving before your brother comes over here wondering why we're just sitting here."

I bit back a sigh and pulled the car out of the spot before making my way out of the parking lot. "I'm sorry, Coen, but you have to understand something. I have avoided men since before Parker was born. I've never wanted a guy in our life, and my family knows that. They don't agree, but they know that. They've tried . . . I don't know how many times over the last six years to get me to start dating. And not once have I even considered it. You saw how pissed off I was when they all went behind my back to set me up on that double date with you. And then you"—I fumbled for my next words and flung my hand out like it would somehow help me find the right thing to say. It didn't. "You were there, and for the first time I actually entertained the thought of being with someone."

Looking over, I was surprised to see him studying me intently. I would have expected him to look smug.

"But, trust me, I tried talking myself out of it so many times. I didn't *want* to want you. Parker and I are fine by ourselves, and throwing a guy into that can just make things so complicated . . . and why complicate things when we're in such a good place now?" I mumbled the last part to myself. "So to go six years of ignoring their attempts at setting me up, and to get Parker and me to a place where we don't need anyone, and then suddenly have there be this guy in the picture?"

"I . . ." Coen huffed. "I still don't get it. Okay, so you didn't want to date a bunch of random guys. Because of that you can't tell them when you're sort of seeing someone? They want you to see people. Your brother tried to set us up. You just said all three of them went behind your back to get us on a double date."

"Yeah, but you don't know my parents, so you didn't see how quickly it all changed. But you had to have noticed how Keegan reacted, and all he knows about is the park."

When he didn't respond, I glanced over at him to see his eyes were narrowed as he watched me.

"When I got pregnant with Parker, I didn't stop going to school. Even after he was born I continued going until I graduated from high school. Granted, I *had* to ask my mom to watch him while I was there because I didn't have a job then. As soon as I graduated I got a job and moved out with Parker six months later. I wanted to put him in day care, but my mom wouldn't let me. I hate not being in control of everything. 'Control' might have been the wrong word . . . I'm not a control freak. It's just . . . if I can't handle something on my own, it scares me. When Austin left me—"

"Austin?"

"Parker's dad. When he left, I was determined to have Parker and be the best mom. I was already having a baby in high school, but I didn't want to be a statistic, you know? So ever since that day when he broke up with me, I have to be able to handle every situation by myself. I don't want to be one of those single moms who constantly has to rely on her family just to get by. Because Austin left us and it was so bad with my parents at first when they found out, I knew I had to be a certain way for Parker. So I hate asking for help. I like knowing I can do it on my own. But my family still thinks they need to watch out for Parker and me. Like they need to protect us because I'm not allowing anyone else to do it. So even though they *want* me to date, bringing someone into Parker's life isn't as easy as *me* thinking he would be good for me, and good to Parker . . . my whole family has to agree."

Coen didn't say anything, and because of the traffic, I couldn't look at him again. Knowing he'd been mad, the quiet was making me uneasy.

"And that was exactly how it all happened tonight. Keegan was looking at you like an enemy instead of his best friend, my dad was sizing you up, my mom . . . God, my mom—"

"She doesn't like the way I look." Coen laughed softly and shifted in the seat. "I noticed."

I grimaced and rubbed at my forehead. "It doesn't matter if she does or doesn't. She obviously got over it. But that's just it . . . to make it all the more confusing. My family—who wanted nothing more than for me to start dating—all about had heart attacks when they thought I was dating someone, and none of them were happy about it. But a couple hours later, my mom is taking my son for the night so I can spend time with you, and I have no doubt she's going to be online picking out my wedding dress once he's asleep." I groaned and slapped my hand back on the steering wheel before I gasped in horror. "Not that we're getting married! Jesus."

Coen's loud laugh filled my car, and I was positive I was bright red.

"God, just . . . act like I didn't say that."

"No can do, Duchess. It's replaying in my head over and over." He laughed when I groaned again, and after a few minutes said, "I get what you're saying, but I'm going to be honest with you. I know we're not really anything yet, but I'm just letting you know now that we won't be anything at all if this is how it's going to be. You being afraid to tell your family about me. You leaving me to answer the questions about us when you look like you're going to throw up because I'm in the same room with them. I'm not gonna deal with that shit."

"Coen, I'm sorry. I hadn't been ready for that and I couldn't figure out what to do. Part of me wanted to go into your arms, and the other part was terrified of how my family was going to react. And I just froze."

He didn't say anything for the next few minutes until I was in the parking lot of his studio, and next to his car. With a hard breath through his nose, he unclicked his seat belt and got out of the car.

My stomach clenched and my head dropped as I realized I'd somehow made this worse. I needed to learn how to shut up. My head snapped to the left when my door opened and he stepped back.

"Get out."

"What?" I looked around the otherwise empty parking lot before looking back at him. "Why?"

"Just get out of the car, Duchess."

I stumbled my way out, and gasped when he pushed me against the back door, pressing both his forearms on the window on either side of my head, caging me in.

"This is where you decide," he said gruffly. "Hudson told me you were independent, and you just told me you get scared if you can't do something by yourself. You didn't have to tell me you don't like people helping you for me to figure that out, but you're not just stopping people from helping you, Reagan. You're stopping anyone except from your family from getting too close. And that includes me."

"But—"

"You're scared, that's fine. But why can't you just see where this goes, huh? For once, let someone else be in control. Let me be there for you, let me help you—" He must have seen the panic in my eyes, because he quickly added, "by just being there for you. Like tonight. Was it so hard for you that I got Parker to eat the rest of his food? Did that make you feel like you didn't have control of the situation? And don't fucking lie to me, I need to know if I messed up by doing—"

"No," I whispered, and realized he was right. The same smile I'd had to cover in the restaurant was back, but this time, I just stood there staring at him in awe. "Watching you two together like that was . . . I don't even know how to describe it, Coen. But not once did it bother me that you were trying to get him to eat. I—to be honest, I loved watching you."

Coen's lips tilted up in a soft smile, and his dark eyes slowly moved over my face. "You need to make the decision. Do you want to try letting me in?" He leaned in close so his breath washed over my lips. "Letting me help you doesn't mean you can't do this alone, Reagan. Everyone knows you can, but you shouldn't have to."

"Coen . . ."

"Yes or no, Duchess."

"Yes," I said without hesitation, and moaned into his mouth when his lips met mine.

Wrapping my arms around his neck, I pulled our bodies closer and groaned my aggravation when his phone rang.

"Yeah?" he answered, and bit down on my bottom lip. "I'm kissing your sister, leave me alone."

"I can't believe you just told him that!" I huffed, and pushed back on his chest.

"Yeah, he's probably going to kick my ass for that one." Capturing my lips with his again, he ran his tongue along mine and whispered, "Don't care. But they're waiting for us at my place, so we should go."

With one last soft, teasing kiss, he pulled back and I asked, "Why?"

"Uh . . . because then he'd just show up here and beat me up?"

I laughed and pushed against his stomach when he stole another kiss. "No, why did you do all this? It hasn't even been a week since we've actually started talking, so why would you put up with me? I know I've embarrassed myself in front of you too many times to count since I first saw you, and we mostly argue, so why would you care to stick around to see what could happen? You could have your pick of girls, ones who wouldn't have kids. I just—I just don't understand why you want to see where this goes so badly."

Coen raised one eyebrow at me. "Don't you?"

"I do, but I'm asking you."

He stayed quiet for a few moments as he thought, and for a while, I didn't think he would answer me. "I don't do relationships, Reagan. I've just never been that guy . . . I've always thought they were pointless, to tell you the truth. I didn't want to deal with the headache of them. And, Duchess, you are proving to be one massive headache that I can't seem to get enough of." He smiled, but it quickly fell.

This was so not going where I thought it'd been about to. "Then why?"

"You want to know why I want this? Why the guy who thinks relationships are a waste of time wants the girl who's scared of them so goddamn bad?" When I nodded, he swallowed hard and looked away for a few seconds. When he finally looked back at me, his face was somber. "Because I found someone who chases away my demons just by looking at me. I had a girl more or less fall into my arms who can make me forget everything just by saying my name. Why wouldn't I push for this?"

My mouth fell open at his words, and I just sat there staring at him. I couldn't figure out a response to such a soul-baring confession, I only knew that I wanted to be her. It didn't matter that I knew he was talking about me; in my mind, I was just Reagan. There was no way for me to be that person to someone else . . . but with the depth of emotion in his words . . . I knew he'd meant every single one of them.

"That is why I want this. That is why I put up with you when you're being unreasonable. That is why—after a week and a half since meeting you—I would do anything to see where we could go. I'm not declaring my love for you, because I'm not in love with you . . . yet. But I've never met anyone like you. And that's not some bullshit line meant to make you fall for me. I never expected to find you; I didn't know someone like you existed. I never knew there could be a relief from the agony I go through every day, and I don't know what I did to deserve it. But after having that relief, after having you near me . . . . Reagan, I crave you. And I can tell you right now it isn't just because you silence my demons. I crave the peace you give me, yeah . . . but I crave your laugh, your love for your son, and *this* more." He cupped his hand around the side of my neck, and my breathing quickened as the place where he was touching warmed. If I looked down, I knew my arms would once again be covered in goose bumps. "You feel that."

It wasn't a question, but I still nodded my head slowly.

He took a deep breath in through his nose, and for the first time since he started explaining to me why he wanted this, his eyes left mine—but only to fall over my face for a few seconds. "Did I just scare you with everything I said?"

"No," I said so softly, I might have only mouthed it.

Coen's lips formed a sad smile, and I cupped his face in my hands.

"You didn't. I hadn't . . . well I don't know what I'd been expecting, but definitely not something that beautiful."

"Beautiful?"

"Yeah, Coen, that was the most beautiful thing anyone has ever said to me. All of it—including the demons."

"You're wondering about them," he guessed.

I shifted my weight and bit down on the inside of my cheek. I didn't want him to think I'd been lying to him, and I didn't want to ruin the moment he'd somehow created with his perfectly haunting words.

"Reagan—"

"Only because of Parker. Coen, I swear when you said that my first thought was I couldn't possibly be the girl you were describing, and I wanted so badly to be her—"

"Just answer. Did. I. Scare you?"

For long seconds, there was no sound except for our breaths as our faces stayed inches apart. Nothing else. The cars on the street, the people walking by—everything else was tuned out as I studied the worry in his dark eyes. "You didn't scare me, but there's something about you that makes me drop my guard, so I need to know: Should I be scared? For Parker . . . should I be scared of your demons, Coen?"

"I'll never do anything to put Parker in danger, and he's not in danger from me. Your brother would never have even considered letting me near you if there was a chance of that. There's just . . . there are things that happened over the years in the army that have stayed with me, and will always stay with me. Things that I wish I'd never seen, things that I can't talk about even still, and some of them your brother doesn't know about. But you don't have anything to be worried about. Okay?"

"I don't like that for you," I whispered, and he laughed humorlessly.

"I don't either, Duchess. But you help."

He started leaning forward to kiss me when his phone went off again. Looking at the screen, he rolled his eyes. "Yes?" Putting a hand between my body and the car, he pulled me forward and turned me to walk toward the driver's seat. "We're leaving right now . . . No I haven't been making out with her this whole time, fuck, Hudson. We were talking . . . Yeah, you know the thing people do when they're getting to know each other? . . . Fuck off, you're not punching me, because your sister's fine, I didn't touch her. We'll be there in a few minutes."

"He won't really punch you," I said when I started my car back up.

"Oh, no. He will. I'm just hoping it's only one hit." He smiled wide before leaning in the open window. "So, are we on the same page now?"

"Yeah, I think so."

He narrowed his eyes before kissing me quickly. "Drive safe, Reagan."

I STAYED AT Coen's for a few hours with Keegan and Erica, and after watching a movie and talking for a while, Keegan and Erica got up to leave. Coen hadn't made a move to let me leave his arms, but Keegan threw me over his shoulder and walked me out to my car, saying I wasn't allowed in Coen's apartment without "Keegan supervision." Oh, and Keegan didn't punch Coen, even though he'd threatened to every time Coen touched or kissed me. Coen still owed me twenty dollars for that. As soon as I was in my apartment, I searched for my phone for twenty minutes before rushing through washing my face and brushing my teeth, and slipping into my pajamas and turning off all the lights and jumping into bed. I sat there trying to calm my breathing, and laughed at how ridiculous I was acting. I'd just spent hours with Coen, and I was still beyond excited for our phone call.

Bringing up his name on my phone, I tapped on the number and played with the ends of my hair as I waited for him to answer.

"Duchess."

A soft breath rushed past my lips at the way his deep voice had my arms covered in goose bumps with just one word. With a shaky breath in, I fell back onto my pillows with a smile on my face—ready to fall asleep to his voice.

Chapter Five

Coen—*August 29, 2010*

REACHING FOR MY phone in the cup holder when it started ringing, I glanced at the name and a smile pulled at my lips. "Beautiful," I said in way of greeting.

She laughed softly. "Delusional?"

"Good to know you still can't take a compliment. What are you up to?"

"Parker's at my parents' again tonight," she said after a few seconds of silence. "My parents wanted to keep him for the night because they want as much time with him as possible before he goes back to school next week. Or that's what they used as an excuse anyway."

My blood heated, and I swear my jeans shrunk. "Are you in need of a distract—shit."

"What?"

"I'm on my way to a shoot, and the guy already

paid me." The second I'd seen her name on my phone, I'd forgotten I was even driving.

"Okay, well, have fun." Her voice had the same sweet softness it always did, but I could hear the disappointment in her words.

This was bad, and it wasn't me. I was getting ready to call off a shoot—something I never did—all because of a girl. "Come with me," I said suddenly.

"What? No, it's fine."

"I'm serious, Reagan, come with me. It's just going to be at my studio."

"Coen"—she laughed softly—"go to your shoot. I'll talk to you later."

"You're going to make me late if you don't get in your car and get your ass over here."

"Oh yeah? And how do you figure that?"

I pulled into the back lot at my studio, but didn't put my car in park as I said, "Because I'm about to turn my car around and come pick you up."

"Do you always get your way?"

"Yeah," I said without hesitation.

After a few moments of silence, she sighed and gave in. "Fine. Fine, I'm on my way."

"See you soon."

I pressed the END button, put the car in park and turned it off before climbing out of it. Knowing Reagan was about to see what I'd given up my career to do, I couldn't stop smiling as I got everything ready for the shoot. My client arrived a handful of minutes later, and after talking more about what he wanted and throwing around some ideas, we started. I tried not to think about the fact that Reagan should have been there ten minutes before. Turning music on as loud as it would go and putting my phone on vibrate so I would know if she called, I tried to focus on my client and what we were going for with this shoot, and not where my mind was wandering to.

By the time the hour-long shoot ended, I was irritated and worried, and had this annoying feeling crawling up the back of my neck. I was trying not to snap at my client and wondering how I'd managed not to break my phone yet.

Reagan hadn't shown, and she hadn't called.

After he left, I flipped through the pictures and was glad I'd somehow managed to get more than enough shots that were perfect for what he wanted, but I felt bad that my client had had to put up with me. As I went through more pictures, I suddenly realized what the annoying feeling was that I'd been having, and my body stilled. Someone was watching me . . . but even as I realized it, I didn't turn around. I knew it was her. I didn't know how I knew, I just did.

"Can I help you?" I asked, never looking up from my camera.

"Get anything good?" Her voice was soft and gentle. Like she didn't care at all that I'd been flipping out for the last hour.

"You could have called."

"Why would I have done that?"

I lowered my hands and lifted my head at the same

time and just stared, seeing nothing, for a few seconds before turning to look at her. "Are you fucking kidding me? I thought you were coming here and you didn't show!"

"I'm here aren't I?" The knowing grin never left her face. "You said you always get your way . . . I had to make sure you didn't this time. Besides, if you really wanted to know if I was coming or not, you could have called me."

Setting my camera down, I began stalking toward her. "I can't just stop a shoot so I can check up on you. You told me you'd be here, I trusted you were coming. Reagan, I've been going out of my mind wondering where you were. I didn't know if you'd gotten in a wreck, if you just decided not to come . . . a thousand possibilities were running through my mind. I was acting like a dick to my client because of you, do you realize that?"

Her smile faltered. "I'm sorry you were worried, honestly I was just waiting for you to turn around . . . and right now, Coen, I'm just playing with you. I've been here for almost an hour, but because you didn't notice me until just now . . . I thought I could tease you about it."

"Don't try to—"

"I'm serious! Call that guy and ask him! I walked in when he was changing into his red shirt, and we waved at each other! I just didn't want to bother you during your shoot, so I waited back here and watched; I'm sorry you got that worried, I didn't know. I kept thinking you would turn around, Coen, I swear to God."

My breathing was ragged, and at some point I'd pinned her up against the back wall. My head understood that she was safe, I could see her, smell her, feel her chest pressed against mine. But my body was still shaking from the amount of adrenaline I had coursing through my veins at the thought of something happening to her, and then her playing me.

Dropping my head, I shook it to the side once and whispered gruffly, "What are you doing to me, Reagan?"

"I don't know wh—I'm sor—do you want me to leave?"

"No, I don't want you to leave. I want to know why you're consuming me this way. I want to know why you're all I can think about. Why the thought of something happening to you, or you standing me up, can completely ruin me like this. I want to know what it is about you that has me so fucking turned around for the first time in my life."

She touched the side of my face and put pressure there until I looked back to her, and when she spoke, her voice was soft and filled with wonder. "I've avoided men for six and a half years, Coen . . . what is it about *you* that has me anxiously waiting for a chance to be near you again?"

I pressed my body closer to hers and dropped my forehead onto hers.

"Everything about you scares me," she admitted quietly.

I ground my jaw and mentally cursed myself for letting her see me frustrated just then. "I didn't mean to scare you, Reagan."

"Don't. You know you and your demons don't scare me." She shook her head slowly. "What you can do to me . . . what you can do to Parker. What letting you into our lives can do to us . . . *that* is what scares me. You have the power to ruin him, Coen, and knowing that makes me want to grab Parker and run."

"Or maybe I'll surprise you," I whispered against her lips. Interlocking our fingers, I raised our hands above our heads and pressed them against the wall. "I respect you for what you've done for him. I respect you for being scared for your son. But I know that if you let me in, I'm getting you and Parker . . . not just you."

Reagan's eyes met and held mine, and I moved both her hands into one of mine and brought my free hand to cup her cheek.

"When I met you, I already knew what you came with. I don't want to see what I can get from you only on nights when your son is gone, Reagan. I want to see what we can be together, and I know that includes your son getting to know me."

"I've never introduced a guy to him," she confessed after a few silent seconds, and I smiled.

"Technically, you've already introduced us, and we already know he likes me." Reagan's eyes narrowed and I brushed my lips across her nose. "You've also never had a guy pursuing you who wasn't afraid of your walls or the fact that you have a son."

"Is that what you're doing?" she asked, and a ghost of a smile crossed her lips. "Pursuing me?"

"Yeah, Duchess. Glad you finally caught on." Pressing my mouth firmly to hers, I teased her lips with my tongue and squeezed my hand tighter around hers when she opened her mouth to me. "Let me surprise you," I begged against her lips.

"I'm waiting," she challenged, and when I looked at the heat in her hazel eyes, I knew the direction of the conversation had changed.

Her breasts moved against my chest with each breath she took, and when I looked down to her parted lips, it was her turn to squeeze my hand from where I still kept them resting high up on the wall. With the hand that had been cupping her cheek, I moved my fingers down her throat, and my lips twitched when I felt her pulse thrumming beneath my fingertips.

Placing my lips on her pulse point, I let my fingers continue a trail down to the low cut of her shirt, and pulled it down even more, revealing her lace-covered breasts. Making a line of openmouthed kisses down the path my fingers had just taken, I took one of her breasts in my mouth and sucked on her hardened nipple through the lace.

Reagan moaned and arched her back against the wall, and her fingers dug into my hand almost to the point of pain when I raked my teeth across her nipple.

"Coen, please," she whimpered. "Touch me."

I let my hand lazily glide down to the top of her shorts, and had just started trying to unbutton them when I remembered where we were. Remembered that I had her pressed against a wall. Releasing her shorts and breast, I moved my mouth back up her chest to her neck, and used my hand to right her shirt.

"Not here," I whispered against her neck.

She pulled back, her eyes wide. "You . . . you want to stop?"

I looked at my studio and shook my head as I released her hands. "I just don't want to do this with you here. Let me take you back to my place."

I'd had meaningless sex in my studio too many times over the years, and the thought of being with Reagan on the same furniture seemed wrong. Like it would cheapen everything about us. Not that there was technically an *us* yet, but she didn't deserve that, and I didn't want that. I wanted somewhere that didn't have drunken one-night memories attached to it.

Grabbing her hand, I shut off the lights in my studio as we walked through it, and locked the door behind us once we were outside. I noticed Reagan grabbing her keys out of her purse and raised an eyebrow at her.

"I just figured I'd follow you," she said, and her cheeks turned red. "You know, so I could leave, um, after or . . . or in the morning."

Biting back a smile, I nodded and pressed a hard kiss to her forehead. "So you plan on staying the night, huh?"

"No, I—"

"I never said that was a bad thing, Duchess."

Reagan's tense body instantly relaxed, and when I pulled away from her she was biting down on the inside of her cheek and her face was red. Fuck, she was adorable.

I walked her to her SUV and waited until she was inside before going to my car and getting in, and as soon as we were on our way to my condo, the direction of my thoughts changed.

Now that I could think clearly without Reagan's body pressed against mine, I knew that taking her back to my place was the wrong move. I'd just told her I was different. I'd just told her I didn't want to see what I could get from her on nights when her son wasn't with her. And yet, the first two nights we were alone—the first two nights we even spent time together—things progressed quickly, and only stopped because of a phone ringing, and the fact that I didn't want to be with her on a couch where I'd fucked random women.

The fact that I could still feel her body against me, the fact that the way she'd softly moaned was still replaying in my mind, and the fact that I was still hard as shit had me wanting to continue the drive to my condo. But I couldn't do this to her.

Pulling over into an Italian restaurant's parking lot, I got out of my car and waited for her to do the same.

"Uh . . . this isn't your place," she said, her confused tone making it sound more like a question.

"I know." I nodded and pulled her into my arms. "But I just told you I wanted to surprise you, and the path we were on was the opposite of that. So I'm going to take you to dinner, and at the end of dinner I'm going to walk you back out here, kiss you good night, and go back to my condo alone."

I held my breath as I waited for her reaction, and told myself again that this was the right thing to do. And as soon as her face lit up in the most beautiful smile I'd ever seen, I knew it had been. Brushing a soft kiss across her lips, I slid my arm around her waist and walked us toward the restaurant.

Reagan—*August 31, 2010*

MY PHONE RANG as I pulled into my parents' driveway, and I couldn't have contained my smile no matter how hard I tried when I saw his name on my screen.

"Hey!"

He laughed quietly. "I love that you don't try to hide the fact that you're excited to talk to me."

I made a face and looked around as I turned off my car. "Uh, that's not a good thing, actually, I'm pretty sure that's embarrassing."

"Don't be embarrassed. Do you know how annoying that whole mysterious, playing hard-to-get voice is? You can never tell if the girl is ready to cry, yell at you, or tear off your clothes. With you, I always know exactly what I'm getting."

I rubbed at my forehead and laughed uneasily. "Okay . . . ? I guess?"

"And I just made this conversation awkward. We're starting this over."

"No! No, we're—Coen? Hello?" I looked at my screen and scoffed. "You really just hung up on me?" I asked when he called back.

"Ooh, pissed off, Duchess."

"I'm not—"

"Hi, Reagan," he said, cutting me off. His deep voice somehow calming and warming every part of my body.

"Hey," I said softly, and smiled as I played with the ends of my hair. "I didn't think I was going to talk to you until later."

"Is that why you were so excited?"

I laughed and covered my face, groaning into my hand. "Yes, that's why I was excited. I'm going to be a robot every time we talk from now on. You'll never have any idea."

"That would be depressing for me."

"And probably impossible for me."

"Uh, yeah. I'd say so. Hey . . . have you gotten Parker yet?"

I went back to playing with the ends of my hair and glanced at my parents' house. "I'm just about to, I'd just pulled in to pick him up when you called."

Coen was silent for a few seconds.

"Why?" I asked, drawing out the word.

"I know you're scared of him getting to know

me . . . but I'd really like to take you and Parker out tonight." When I didn't respond, his voice filtered through the phone again, his tone now borderline worried. "Reagan?"

"Um," I began, and licked my lips. "Well . . ."

I looked toward the house again as I tried to come up with an excuse. *I have work tomorrow. True. I have to do laundry. Not true. I have to clean. Unfortunately true, but I won't get to it tonight regardless. I have to watch my plant grow. I don't have any plants. I need more time to sit here playing with my hair while I think of a really good reason not to go!* I straightened in my seat and stared at my steering wheel as I thought. Just last week I hadn't been ready for the three of us to hang out, but I also hadn't known how serious Coen was about this relationship—and he was right: Parker already adored him.

With school starting in less than a week, the only time I'd be alone without Parker would be the Fridays my work was closed . . . I knew this needed to happen soon, or eventually I would start thinking of reasons for us not to be together because of the time apart.

"We can wai—"

"What'd you have in mind?"

There was a heavy silence before Coen added softly, "Don't do this if you're not ready."

"You already know him, Coen, I'm just being dumb."

"No, you're not. You're protecting your son."

I smiled and thought again about Coen getting Parker to eat. My dad couldn't even do that. "I'm unnecessarily protecting him from someone he already knows and likes, and someone I'm dating and kinda, maybe, sorta like too."

"Kinda, maybe, sorta," he said, his voice monotone.

"Yeah," I teased. "So what did you want to do tonight?"

"We can do easy. We can just grab dinner. Or we can—"

"Easy sounds good."

"All right, easy it is. Can I pick you both up in an hour?"

I bit down on the inside of my cheek and shifted uncomfortably in my seat. "Can we meet you wherever you want to eat? Unless you want me to pick you up? Otherwise I have to move the booster seat to your car and it'll just be weird."

"Booster seat?"

"Yep . . . problems you'll come across dating a mom."

"I don't ever remember being in one of those."

I laughed and stepped out of my car. "I can't remember it either, but it's the law now."

"Seriously?"

"Yeah, Steele, seriously."

He paused before saying, "Don't call me that. It's weird."

"Don't call me Duchess."

Coen drew out a groan. "I'm not sure if I can commit to that."

"Well then, that's your problem, not mine. I have to get Parker, text me where you want us to meet you."

"You don't play fair, Duchess."

"Neither do you, Steele. See you soon." I grinned and tapped END before opening the door and almost running into my brother. "Hey! I thought you were moving into your apartment with Erica."

He pulled me into a hug and moved me away from the door so he could shut it. "I am, we've been moving all day. I just ran back here to get the last truckfull. Erica's been unpacking all day, so it actually looks decent. You wanna come by tonight and see it? I'll order pizza."

"I can't. Parker and I have something going on tonight."

"Like . . . ?"

"Um . . ."

"Well, shit, Ray! You're playing with your hair, so now you're freaking me the fuck out. Tell me what it is."

"Keegan!" I hissed, and smacked his arm as I looked around for my son. "Do you have to cuss in front of Parker?"

He cringed for a split second before relaxing. "No, we're good. He's out back with Mom. Now, tell me what you're doing tonight."

Dropping my hair, I straightened my back and tried to look directly into my brother's eyes. It didn't work. He's eight inches taller than me. "Coen's taking us to dinner."

"Coen's taking you *and* Parker to dinner?"

"Yes, he is, and why do you look like that? I don't understand you. Why would you try to set me up with your best friend if you would ever have this worried look on your face! I know you told me you didn't think we'd actually date, but come on, Keegan. Tell me why you're acting like this! Is there something I should know? Something I should be worried about?"

"No," he huffed and rolled his eyes. "No. Steele's one of the best guys I know."

I shrugged and put my hands up to the sides of my head before dropping them. "Then *what*? I don't understand!"

Keegan looked past me for a while before clearing his throat and asking, "Does he sleep?"

"What?"

"When he's, uh, with you. Does he sleep?" he gritted out, and then mumbled to himself, "I'll kill the bastard for touching you."

"What? Keegan! No, we haven't done anything! He's kissed me, that's all. But even if we had, I wouldn't tell you about it."

Keegan sighed in relief and I crossed my arms over my chest.

"No killing Coen. And don't punch him either."

"I'm not promising the last one. No fucking way."

"Keegan—"

"Ray!"

"Whatever!" I groaned, and ran a hand through my hair agitatedly. "Tell me why you wanted to know if he slept."

"I—" he cut off and breathed out heavily through his nose. "It's not my story to tell you. The only reason I'm worried is, well, other than the obvious of you being my little sister, and Parker being my nephew, and I would be worried no matter what. But, I know Steele's seen some things, and I know that it's fucked him up—"

"His demons," I whispered.

"What?"

"He told me something about that the other night before we met up with you and Erica at his condo, when you kept calling us." Keegan just stared at me like he was waiting for me to continue. "Keegan, it was kind of personal."

"Reagan. My guy told you about his demons, and you're not gonna tell me what he said, and you expect me to let you take my nephew to dinner with him?"

I rolled my eyes and huffed. "He said I could silence his demons just by looking at him. He said it was because of his time in the army, about things during that time that he couldn't tell me."

Keegan no longer looked worried, or like the big, protective older brother. He looked shocked. "He said that to you?" he asked softly.

I nodded. "Why?"

He looked down, and a small smile crossed his face as he nodded softly. "Good for him," Keegan said as he turned and walked toward the stairs.

I just stood there staring at his back, completely dumbfounded for a few seconds before I took a step toward him. "Wait, so you're just okay with this now?"

When he looked back at me, he looked like he was trying to figure out what to say, and finally just shrugged. "Yeah, Ray. What he told you that night . . . that's about as honest as he can get with what happened, and what's going on with him. Knowing that he's not keeping anything from you . . . and having seen how good he is with Parker. I think you're just as good for him as he is for you."

I was still staring at where Keegan had been when Parker came racing through the house. "Mom!"

"Hey, baby! Did you have fun today?"

"So much fun!" Parker launched into a play-by-play of their day, and I tried not to laugh when my mom walked in behind him and rolled her eyes before smiling.

"That crazy, huh?"

"Oh, it was nonstop today," she said. "Did you want to stay for dinner?"

I shifted on my feet for a second before glancing down at Parker. "We can't. Coen's taking us to dinner tonight." I'd barely looked up to see Mom's reaction when Parker jumped up in front of me.

"Me too?"

I smiled widely at him. "You too, buddy."

"No way! Come on, Mom, let's go!"

"Okay, just a second, let me talk to Grandma first." Looking up at my mom, my body tightened when I couldn't read her expression. "Too soon?"

"We liked him." She shrugged. "He does have an awful lot of tattoos, though. You don't want Parker thinking those are okay."

I suppressed a groan. "Mom. Really? Keegan has tattoos."

"Not like that."

"Mom!"

"Okay, okay!" She held her hands up. "We did like him. Despite the tattoos," she threw in. "He seems like a wonderful young man. Keegan had a lot of great things to say about him when we asked him, but, I would trust his judgment on this."

It was there, on that last bit that I realized Keegan must have told my parents his worries about Coen and his demons. Whatever they were. I could see it in my mom's eyes. She was worried about this too, just as Keegan had been. But she didn't understand, she didn't know Coen. What was I saying? *I* barely knew Coen.

"I approve," Keegan said as he appeared from out of nowhere.

I pointed at him. "He approves!"

"You do?" Mom asked, eyeing him warily.

"One hundred percent. I think he'd be good for them, and she'd be good for him."

Turning, I sent him a thankful smile, and he winked at me as he opened the front door and walked out. Looking back at my mom, I saw her blink a few times before clapping her hands together once.

"Well, since I just put it all on Keegan, I guess that settles that."

"It'll be fine, Mom," I said, hoping to reassure her. "You ready to go, buddy?"

Parker was studying his forearm intently, so he just nodded as he started walking toward the front door. "Mommy, do you think Coen will still have his stars?"

My eyes widened and I turned to look at my mom. "Uh, yeah, Parker. He will."

"Because he's old so his won't wash away."

"Right."

"I'm gonna get old so mine won't wash away, because I'm getting stars just like Coen's."

Mom groaned and rolled her eyes, and I tried covering my laugh with a cough, and failed miserably. Blowing her a kiss, I put my hand on Parker's back and led him outside.

"Why don't we wait a decade or so until we think about that, okay? Right now, let's just go have dinner with Coen, sound good?"

"Cool!"

I smiled and followed my son to the car. The entire time I chanted to myself that this dinner was a good idea. That one day I wouldn't regret letting my guard down for a guy like Coen and letting him into my son's life.

Chapter Six

Coen—*September 2, 2010*

"THIS IS THE coolest, ever!" Parker yelled. "Coen's the coolest, isn't he, Mom?"

I glanced over at Reagan and she rolled her eyes at me. "Yeah, he's pretty cool, buddy."

"And this one comes off because I'm not old like you?"

I barked out a laugh and kept pressing the wet paper towel down on Parker's arm. "That's right, bud. It'll come off in a few days."

I held the paper towel there for a few more seconds before removing it, and then removed the hard back for the temporary tattoo and watched as Parker's eyes lit up.

"Cool!"

I'm positive *cool* was his favorite word, and the extent of expressive words at that. But I had to steal his word. This kid was pretty damn cool.

"What do you think?" I held out his arm so Reagan could see, and even though she shot me a look, a smile crossed her face.

"Mom, isn't it cool?"

"So cool, Parker."

"I can't wait to show Jason!" he said excitedly before tearing out of Reagan's kitchen to go back to playing in the living room.

My lips slowly curved up into a smile as Reagan fought and lost with biting back her own smile, and I pulled her close. "You mad at me?"

She looked up at me and wrapped her arms around my neck. "Mad? Are you kidding? I'm furious," she whispered.

"You look it," I murmured against her lips and she smiled against my kiss.

"That was really sweet of you," she said when I pulled back. "He doesn't even remember they're called tattoos, but all he talks about are the stars on your arm. They're the only ones he remembers. This was . . ." she floundered for something to say as she looked over at Parker. "This was fun for him. I already know he's going to talk about that tattoo, and who gave it to him, until it washes off." Looking back at me, she shrugged. "Thank you."

"Not a big deal. He spent the whole night talking about it the other night, had to get one for him."

Her hazel eyes held mine, and her lips tilted up on one side. "That's just it. You didn't have to."

"Okay, I *wanted* to. Better?"

"Much."

I leaned in, and had just barely brushed my lips against hers when we heard, "Ew, you're kissing a girl?"

Reagan froze, and I held back a laugh as I turned my head to look at Parker. "Yeah, why, do you want me to kiss a boy?"

Parker made a face. "Gross! No! But girls have cooties!"

"Yeah? Says who?"

His mouth opened and his eyebrows pinched together for a few seconds before he sputtered, "Everyone."

I unwrapped my arms from Reagan, and crouched down so I was his height. "Girls your age *do* have cooties," I whispered loudly, and tried so hard not to smile when he nodded quickly. "But you know how I'm old so my stars don't wash off?" Parker looked at his star, then my tattoos before nodding again. "Well, when you're this old, girls don't have cooties anymore. So they're safe to kiss."

Parker looked at me like he was trying to memorize every word I was saying. "How will I know when they're safe?"

I glanced up at Reagan, and her face fell into a look of horror. "He's six," she mouthed.

"Just trust me on this, bud," I said when I looked back at Parker. "You'll know."

"'Kay," he replied, and looked up at Reagan. "It's okay, Mom. You're safe, you won't give Coen cooties."

My head dropped so he wouldn't see how hard I was trying not to laugh, but I knew my shoulders were shaking from trying to hold it back.

"Thanks for that, buddy. Why don't you go wash your hands so we can eat, all right?"

"Okay!"

I straightened, my body still shaking from the laughs I'd been trying so hard to quiet, and Reagan punched my shoulder as soon as I was upright.

"Seriously?"

"Hey! At least I told him the girls his age had cooties."

A laugh bubbled past her lips before she could contain it, and then her stern expression was back. "But now what if he avoids women until he's like thirty?"

"He won't. Trust me, once puberty hits you'll be wishing he would avoid them until he was thirty. At least I bought you a few years. I could've told him cooties didn't exist and you'd have the principal calling you because he was kissing all the girls in his class next week. I know from experience."

A sly grin crossed her face. "Coen Steele, did you terrorize all the girls by kissing them?"

I shrugged as I grabbed the food and started walking toward the table. "Someone had to do it. I took one for the team."

"Ah, must have been such a hardship."

"You have no idea."

Reagan just smiled and shook her head as she

leaned up to press her lips to my jaw. "And are you
still terrorizing them all?"

"Just one," I whispered.

"Good answer."

REAGAN SHUT THE door leading to Parker's bedroom,
and smiled up at me as she easily fell into my arms
where I stood leaning against the wall.

"He is *out*," she whispered, and pressed her lips to
my throat as she wrapped her arms around my neck.
"Tonight was fun for him."

"It was fun for me too," I said honestly.

After dinner, we'd watched a movie before playing
a game for hours that I still didn't understand . . . and
I already wanted another night like the one we'd just
had.

My fingers flexed against her hips when her mouth
pressed firmly against mine, and a soft whimper
sounded in her throat when our tongues brushed
against each other. Moving my legs apart, I pulled
her closer against me, and she arched her back so
her chest pushed into mine for a few moments before
moving back. Her hands slowly moved from my neck,
across my chest and down my stomach before resting
on the top of my jeans. The muscles in my abdomen
twitched when her fingers moved under the shirt to
brush against my skin.

I knew I needed to stop this. I'd told her I wanted
to surprise her, and somehow we always found our-

selves here . . . with me trying to find the will to be the voice of reason for us . . . for her. For her, I needed to stop this. I needed to show her I wanted so much more from her. But when she flattened one hand against my lower stomach, and the other curled around the top of my already low-slung jeans, I forgot all the reasons why I'd stopped us before.

Pushing off the wall, I took the few steps until her back hit the opposite wall, and released her lips to make a trail down her throat. Pushing aside the collar of her shirt, I placed slow kisses across her collarbone as I pressed a hand to the small of her back, bringing her body closer to mine.

One of her hands went up to run over my short hair when I bit down gently on her neck, and she gasped softly before whispering, "I want to fall asleep to your voice tonight."

I stilled and pressed a kiss to where I'd bitten her before moving back so I could look into her eyes. Cocking my head to the side, I pushed some of her hair behind her ear. "You do every night, why wouldn't you tonight?"

"No, uh . . ." She put one hand to my chest, as if to push me away, and grabbed the ends of her hair with the other.

"What, Reagan, tell me." *Shit, I'd pushed her too far.* "I'm sorry, I should've left as soon as you went to put—"

"Coen, no." She stopped me by pressing three fingers to my lips. Moving them away, she brushed her lips softly across mine, and when her eyelids slowly opened, they revealed a heat in her hazel eyes. "I want to fall asleep to your voice . . . while you're in my bed."

"Duchess," I said darkly.

Pushing back on my chest so she could move away from the wall, she grabbed one of my hands and began walking backward down the hall. "Please don't leave."

"Staying could be dangerous." I warned her. "I don't think I'd be able to stop us this time."

She smiled when we stepped into her room and let go of my hand to press hers to my stomach again. Her eyes flickered down to watch as her fingers moved along the inside of my jeans. "Maybe you shouldn't stop us anymore."

I bit down on the inside of my cheek and took a deep breath in and out. My first thought was to grab her and take her to the bed, but I had to make sure she wouldn't regret this tomorrow.

"Reagan, don't do this for me," I said, my voice coming out rough from trying to restrain myself.

She bit back a smile and looked up at me. "Stop thinking you're pushing me into something I'm not ready for. I want this." A look of uncertainty crossed her face, and her hand stilled. "Unless you don—"

Grabbing the back of her head, I slammed my mouth down onto hers and growled, "Don't finish that thought. You'd be out of your goddamn mind to think I don't want you."

Walking us toward the bed, I grabbed the bottom

of her shirt and pulled it over her head—letting the
material fall to the floor as I pushed her a step away.
My eyes moved over her body, and snapped up to hers
when her hands went to her back to undo the clasp on
her bra.

Closing the distance between us again, I put my
hands on her hips and led her back until her legs hit
the bed. She stumbled onto it with a husky laugh, and
I moved my hands to her bare knees. Parting them
enough so I could step between her legs, I watched as
she moved the straps of the bra off her shoulders and
down her arms. As soon as it was on the floor with
her shirt, her hands went to cover herself, and her legs
tried to close as the most beautiful blush I've ever seen
stained her cheeks.

Moving one of my hands to where she was holding her breasts, I grabbed at her wrists and moved her
resisting arms away from her body as I laid her down
on the bed.

Resting our hands above her head, I brushed my
lips against her softly, and asked, "Where'd my fear-
less girl go?"

Her lips trembled against mine when she responded. "Its one thing to start it—and to feel confident. Its another when there's nothing to hide behind
anymore."

I moved back enough to look into her eyes, and
shook my head softly. "Don't hide yourself with me.
Do you know how beautiful you are?"

Kissing her until I felt her body begin to relax

under mine, I slowly moved down her neck and chest until I reached the swell of her breast. With the hand still on her knee, I ran it up her thigh, taking her short and loose skirt with me, until I was gripping her hip through the bunched-up material. Pulling one of her nipples into my mouth, I smiled against her when her back arched and her fingers gripped my hand—just like she'd done when we'd been in my studio.

Sitting back on my knees, I moved down her breast and over to the other to pay the same attention, and released her hip to let my fingers trail under the part of the skirt that was still covering her. I moved over the insides of her legs, and the top of her underwear, but never closer until she started restlessly moving on the bed.

"Coen, *please*."

Grabbing the lace covering her, I pulled it down, and over her legs—letting her move them the rest of the way off as I trailed my fingers over her wet heat. Reagan pressed against my hand and moaned when I made teasing circles against her clit.

"Let me touch you," she pleaded as she tried to free her arms.

The second I released her, she was pulling on my shirt, and unbuttoning my pants as soon as the shirt hit the floor. I laughed against her frustrated whimper when she couldn't move my pants down, and stood off the bed for a second to rid myself of them and the boxer briefs. Her eyes widened as they moved over my body, and something in me halted when I removed her skirt.

"Reagan." I said her name like a prayer, and my hands trailed over her as I came to rest between her legs again. "You're fucking perfection."

Her eyes met mine, and a slow smile crossed her flushed face. Bringing one hand to the back of my neck, she pulled me toward her, meeting me halfway, and pressed her lips to mine. Pushing two fingers inside her, I swallowed her moans as I laid her back on the bed.

"You're perfection . . . and you're mine," I mumbled against her lips.

She smiled, but it fell into a look I knew I never wanted to forget as I teased her clit and moved my fingers inside her. Her head dropped back on the mattress, and her body arched against mine as she ground her hips into my hand. When she began tightening around me, I removed my fingers, and just as she started to protest the loss of them, pushed into her as I quickened my pace on her clit.

Her eyes widened and a sharp cry left her mouth as her orgasm tore through her body, and I stilled as I felt her simultaneously stretching, and tightening and trembling around my cock.

"Coen! Oh God!"

I smiled against her neck before nipping on it gently, and gripping her hip as I began moving inside her. Her legs wrapped around my back as her body continued to tremble, and a moan left her when I bent to pull one of her nipples into my mouth again. She dug her nails into my back and gasped as I raked my teeth over her nipple before sucking it back into my mouth.

"Too hard?" I asked against her soft skin.

"No," she said breathlessly. "Don't stop."

I pushed harder into her as I licked and sucked on her nipple, before biting down and raking my teeth over it. Each time she'd clench around my cock, and each time she'd whimper when I licked it once more before blowing cool air on it and moving to the next one.

"Oh God. I think . . ."

Moving so I was on my knees and resting on one of my elbows, I moved my hand down to where our bodies were joined, and the next time I bit down on her nipple, I pinched her clit—and her body exploded around mine. Reagan screamed, and I moved my hand away to cover her mouth as I rode her through her orgasm. Her eyes locked on mine as she continued to moan against my hand, and her fingers dug so hard into my back that I had no doubt I'd have marks when I stilled above her as my release came.

Her breathing was ragged, and soft whimpers were sounding in her chest when I removed my hand, but the most beautiful smile crossed her face.

"Are you okay?" I asked roughly as I held my body above hers.

She looked at me for long seconds before finally

nodding, her smile somehow softening into a look even more beautiful. "More than okay."

I breathed a sigh of relief and pressed my mouth to hers twice before backing up enough to look into her eyes. "I'm sorry for cov—"

"Don't, I know why you did," she said as understanding crossed her face. "But I wouldn't stop you from doing that even if he wasn't here."

My face fell, and somehow, impossibly, I was ready to go again. "You will be the death of me, Reagan Hudson, I have no doubt of that."

She smiled and leaned up to capture my lips with hers before pulling me down with her. "Then I'll just have to be careful with you," she said as she bit down on my bottom lip.

Smirking, I moved to brush my nose along her jaw. "I wouldn't go that far, Duchess."

Reagan—*September 3, 2010*

MY EYELIDS SLOWLY blinked open, and for a second my body froze. The feel of a heavy arm draped over my waist, a body pressed against my back, and a nose barely grazing the back of my neck wasn't something I'd ever had before. Even with Austin. And once the initial shock of having someone in my bed wore off, and trying to wake up enough to figure out who it was before I started screaming that there was some creeper in my bed, I lay there trying to memorize the way this felt.

I'd never felt as safe, wanted, or perfectly happy as I did in that moment.

When I remembered last night, a smile tugged at my lips and I curled my body deeper into Coen's arms. His fingers tightened against my stomach, and his nose rubbed against the back of my neck before his lips gently followed.

My smile widened and I moved my hands behind me to run them over his buzzed head. "Good morning."

"Mo—wait, what time is it?" his gruff voice asked.

"Uh, about 5:30?"

Coen was silent for so long that I rolled over so I was now on his chest, and looking into his wide eyes.

"What's wrong—I thought we'd agreed you were staying . . . ?"

"It's five thirty?"

I just nodded. I didn't understand why he was looking at me like he was. Like I'd just given him the most amazing gift. If anything, I thought he'd be mad I'd woken him up so early.

"Coen . . ."

He huffed and he flashed a quick smile. "I slept," he replied, and shrugged.

"Uh, yeah?"

Shaking his head quickly, he smiled at me and cupped my face in his hands before kissing me thoroughly. "That was the best sleep I've had in . . . in years."

I smiled against his lips and kissed him again. "Really?"

"Yeah, Reagan. Really."

I kind of wanted to say something like "best sleep ever," but just then Coen began teasing my tongue with his own, and all thoughts of actual conversation died.

Positioning myself better so I was fully on top of him, I spread my legs slowly until my knees were pressed against the mattress and I was straddling him. Coen growled into my mouth when his hardening cock pressed against my core, and I rocked myself against him—craving the feel of him.

"Reagan," he said my name in warning. "You're loud."

I smiled. "And you know how to shut me up."

The sound of approval in his chest had my insides heating faster. Gripping my hips, he moved me up and slowly slid me back down his length as he asked, "How long until Parker wakes up?"

I whimpered, and it took Coen asking me again before I finally responded. "An hour," I said breathily.

"Perfect."

I SMILED AGAINST Coen's kiss almost an hour later as he passed me to pick his shirt up off the floor and pull it over his head. My eyes followed the shirt as it covered up his lean muscles and tattoos, and I frowned now that he was fully clothed.

"Keep looking at me like that, Duchess, and I'm

taking you back to bed," he said huskily, his eyes never once meeting mine.

After last night, and then again in the bed and shower this morning, there should be no way I could even think about that. Just once with him, after six and a half years without anyone, had left me aching in the most amazing way. But even still, a heat started deep in my stomach and my arms were covered in goose bumps as a shiver worked its way up my spine.

Coen looked over at me before doing a double take. A smirk tugged at his lips as he walked over to me to brush a kiss against my neck. "Your son is going to wake up. As much as I want to spend all day with you . . . *in* you . . . it's time to get dressed."

From the deep laugh that burst from his chest when he moved away, I'm pretty sure I was pouting like a three-year-old. Picking up the shirt I'd dropped as I'd watched him dress, I put it on and thought of something for the first time since I'd asked Coen to stay the night.

"Parker . . ."

Coen raised an eyebrow at me and looked toward the door for a second. "I didn't hear anything."

"No, I just . . . I didn't think about this."

Understanding washed over his face. "About him waking up, and me being here . . . in the same clothes?"

I nodded and bit down on the inside of my cheek. "But I doubt he'd notice your clothes. If he had it his way, he'd wear the same thing every day of the year."

Coen smiled and walked closer to me. Holding out his hand, he waited until I put my hand in his before pulling me toward him. "Don't take this the wrong way, Reagan, but I think it's way too early for him to find me here in the morning. Too soon for him, too soon for our relationship . . ."

"Good!" I blew out a relieved breath and moved so I was pressed against his chest. "I think it is too. I'm happy you stayed last night, and if you ever want to, I want you to stay again. But I don't think Parker should know that yet."

His dark eyes showed just how glad he was that we were both on the same page with this. "So, should I leave through the window or . . ." he teased, and kissed me quickly when I laughed and pushed against his chest.

"We'll just have to be quiet," I whispered, and winked at him as I led him from my bedroom and through the hallway. When we got to my front door, I looked up into his dark eyes and was already wishing for another night with him. "Thank you for staying."

That look was back. Like I'd just given him the most amazing gift. I didn't understand it. But if I got kisses like the one he gave me just then every time he looked at me like that, then I'd want to get that look all the time. "Thank *you*," he said softly when the kiss ended. "Have a good day, Reagan."

"You too." I watched him walk out to his car, and as soon as he was in it, shut the door and tried to school my expression before waking up Parker.

Walking into his room, I smiled when I found him starfished on his stomach, his temporary tattoo on display.

"Wake up, honey," I crooned softly as I rubbed his back. "Parker, wake up."

He rolled his head to the side and looked up at me sleepily.

"Morning."

"Hi, Mom." He did a weird little wave before gasping and sitting up on his knees and looking around.

"What's wrong?"

"Where's Coen?"

My body froze. Had he heard us? *Oh God.* My stomach filled with dread at that thought. "He's at his house, baby."

When Parker looked at me again, he was disappointed. "Oh."

I licked my lips quickly and had to look away for a second as I tried to compose myself. "Why did you think he'd be here?"

Parker shrugged and looked down at his lap as he mumbled something.

"Don't mumble."

"He's gonna come back, right?"

I smiled at my son, and was so glad he liked Coen just as much as I did. "Of course he is."

Parker's face lit up and he bounced up and down. "Is he gonna be my dad?!"

"What?" I managed to choke out.

It felt like all the air had left my body. I wasn't sure I remembered how to even pull more into my body. *Breathe, Reagan, breathe. How do I breathe?!*

"Why would you ask that?" I tried to keep the horror from my tone, but I knew I hadn't succeeded. Parker didn't seem to notice either way. He still looked beyond excited.

"Because Jason has a dad, and he said everyone has a dad. But I don't. Uncle Keegan's my uncle. And Grandpa is my grandpa. And I like Coen. So can Coen be my dad, Mom?"

"Um . . ." *Is twenty-two too early to start having hot flashes?* "Parker—"

"I'm going to ask him if I can start calling him 'Dad' next time I see him!"

Parker jumped off his bed and began running around the room as he tore off the shirt he'd slept in, and threw it on the bed.

"Parker, baby, I need you to understand something." I waited for him to stop running around and look at me until I spoke again. "Coen can't just start *being* your dad, do you understand?"

His forehead scrunched together like he was trying really hard to.

I wasn't about to explain adoption to him, so I skipped to something easier. "If Coen and Mommy got married, then Coen would be your dad."

Parker laughed. "Okay, Mom! You can marry him, because he's going to be my dad!" He held up an imaginary light saber—sounds and all—and started using it as he ran out of his room. "Can we have waffles?" he yelled from down the hall.

"Oh God," I groaned, and dropped my face into my hands.

I thought back to Coen's words and my blood ran cold. *"Don't take this the wrong way, Reagan, but I think it's way too early for him to find me here in the morning. Too soon for him, too soon for our relationship . . ."*

Of course all this was too soon. Too soon. Too soon. And if Parker told Coen that he wanted Coen to be his dad . . . this was too soon for *me*!

Oh Jesus. I jumped up from Parker's bed and ran to the guest bathroom as my body mercilessly tried to throw up anything. Dry heaves continued to torment my body for minutes until my stomach calmed, and I sat back to find Parker standing there looking scared.

"I'm fine."

He nodded, but just kept staring at me.

"See? All better." I smiled and stood from my spot on the floor to reassure him, and finally he nodded hard twice.

"Yeah, well, when Coen's my dad he can make sure you're better."

My stomach churned again. "Buddy. You—I don't think you should tell Coen that you want him to be your dad."

"No, its okay, Mom. He wants to be." Grabbing

my hand, he pulled me out of the bathroom. "Come on, I'll make you waffles so you'll be better."

He couldn't make waffles. And I wasn't sure if I could eat. But I loved my son, and I loved his heart. I was just terrified of what his wants for Coen in our lives was going to *actually* do to Coen in our lives.

Chapter Seven

Reagan—*September 3, 2010*

I GLANCED ANXIOUSLY over to my left, as I had so many times this morning, and tried not to lose what little breakfast I'd managed to eat when I saw Coen running in this direction off in the distance. I hadn't told Coen we would be here, I'd just hoped he would have called if he was going to show up. Looking back at the playground, I easily found where Parker and Jason were playing together and tried to stay focused on them instead of seeming like I was avoiding Coen.

Which I was.

"Morning," he said through heavy breaths as he came to a stop near me.

"Mmm" was my only response as I tried not to eye him standing there.

"Um . . . are you just going to act like you can't see

me now?" he asked a couple minutes later when I still hadn't said anything to him.

I turned toward him, my eyebrows bunching together. "I said good morning, didn't I?"

He laughed hard once and eyed me curiously. "Are you okay?"

I huffed and turned to face the playground again. "I'm making sure Parker's safe."

"Hmm . . ." Coen mused next to me. "Sitting on the concrete playing with figurines. That's some dangerous shit right there."

"Language, Coen." I groaned and rolled my eyes as I faced him again. "And like we've declared, you don't have kids, so you don't know how fast something can go wrong."

"Coen!"

We both turned at Parker's voice and Coen braced himself just in time for Parker to launch himself at Coen. "What's up, bud?"

"Did you come to play?"

"Not today, I was just on a run and thought I'd come say hi. Are you having fun?"

"Yeah!" Parker said excitedly and threw his arm straight out in front of him and pointed at the temporary tattoo. "And everyone thinks I'm the coolest because I'm just like you now."

Coen's smile widened and he held up his fist for Parker to hit it. "You do look pretty cool, bud. I'm not gonna lie. If it stays on through next week, you'll be the coolest first grader too."

My chest warmed watching them interact, and I felt my lips spread into the most ridiculous smile. Remembering this morning, the smile quickly fell from my face and I crossed my arms over my chest—as if that could ward off the warmth I felt watching them together.

"Are you coming over again soon?"

Coen shrugged and nodded toward me. "I don't know, that's up to your mom."

"Mom, can Coen come over again?"

Looking over at me, Coen lowered his voice so Parker couldn't hear him. "Yeah, Reagan . . . can I come over again?"

I didn't miss the suggestive tone in his question, and just as I was about to give him a look telling him to cool it in front of Parker, he started wrapping his arm around my waist, and I jumped away from him. Coen's arm fell, as did his expression before confusion settled over his face.

"Uh, we'll see, honey. Why don't you go back to playing with Jason . . . unless you're ready to leave?"

"No, Mom, please? Can we stay longer?"

I just nodded and smiled until he turned and ran back to where Jason was still sitting, and sighed in relief—knowing we'd gotten through a conversation without Parker mentioning the dad thing.

"Hey," Coen said softly, and reached for my hand. "What's wrong?"

"Stop," I hissed, and moved away from him.

Coen looked at me in shock, his mouth slightly open as he tried to find the words to say. "Rea—"

"You can't just touch me like that in front of Parker," I whispered, and looked around to see if anyone was near us.

Coen's eyebrows shot up, and he blinked slowly at me. "You're . . . you're joking, right?"

"No, I'm not. He'll start getting used to seeing that, and I don't want him to."

"Are you—I don't fucking understand where all this is coming from, Reagan. Just last night I kissed you in front of him. Fuck, *you* kissed *me* in front of him. You were lying in my arms in front of him while we watched the movie. And now all of a sudden I can't put my arm around you? I can't hold your damn hand? Something I did the first night we all hung out together? What has changed since last night that I don't know about?"

I swallowed past the lump in my throat, and focused on Parker instead of Coen. "I just think that all of this is too much. You spending time with us, being around Parker, him getting used to you . . ."

He laughed and ran a hand over his head, but there was an edge to the laugh. He knew I was shutting him out, and from the look in his eyes, he was terrified. "Isn't that the point? For him to get used to me? For him to get to know me? For me to get to know him? All of this as a part of wanting to be with his mom?"

Locking my jaw when I saw his confused and hurt

expression, I tried to find the will to say what was needed, but the words wouldn't come.

"Tell me what happened. Tell me what that mind of yours is scaring you with now, Reagan. Because I went to your apartment for the first time last night, something I know you don't let anyone do. I spent time making dinner and watching a movie with you and your son." Coen closed the distance between us and gritted, "When he went to sleep, I was buried so deep inside you I had to keep my hand over your fucking mouth so he wouldn't hear you screaming."

"Coen!" I scolded, and searched wildly to make sure no one could hear us.

"You begged me to stay with you, and last night was the best. Night. Of my damn life. You and I both agreed Parker seeing me in the morning was too soon. And I've only been gone from you for four hours. So, tell me. What am I missing?"

"I just realized that all of this was too much. Okay? It's all going too fast for me, and I'm not ready for this. I never wanted a relationship; or have you already forgotten that? I don't want you in our life, Coen."

Coen's body went rigid, and his mouth slowly opened as he stared at me. "Bullshit," he breathed.

I felt sick. But I needed to do this now. I needed to do this before we got more attached and he ran, and I had no doubt, especially if he heard Parker calling him "Dad", he would run. "I'm sorry, Coen."

He shook his head back and forth as he continued to watch me. Glancing over at Parker, his forehead

pinched together and a sadness fell over his features
before they hardened and he looked back at me. "Hope
I was a good distraction for you, Reagan."

A huff of air blew past my lips. It felt like I'd been
punched in the stomach, but I couldn't stop him from
leaving. *This needs to be done. The sooner the better. You're
doing the right thing for Parker.*

Without another word, Coen turned and started
running back toward his condo, and my chest ached.
How had this man fallen into our lives, and so quickly
embedded himself in my son's and my heart? Looking
back at Parker, I continued to chant to myself that I'd
done the right thing, but nothing about what had just
happened, or the loss I currently felt, felt like the right
thing.

"KEEGAN, PLEASE BE home," I whispered to myself as
I knocked on the door of his apartment a few hours
later.

"Where are we?"

Glancing down at Parker, I tried to smile and keep
my tone light as I said, "Uncle Keegan's new apartment."

"All right! I get to show him how I'm just like Coen
now!" he said excitedly, and looked down at his arm,
and I bit down on my cheek to stop the agonized cry
from leaving me.

"Keegan," I groaned, and knocked harder.

"Ray, what the—hey, little man!" Keegan sent me

a hard look before smiling down at Parker and holding his hand up for Parker to slap.

"Is Erica here?" I asked anxiously.

"Uh . . . yeah?"

"Can she watch Parker while I talk to you?"

"Uh, Ray—"

"Hey, Parker!" Erica came around Keegan and held out her hand for Parker. "Come hang out with me for a little bit."

"Look what Coen gave me!" Parker said and held out his arm.

Erica and Keegan shared a look before Erica smiled at him again. "That's awesome! Come tell me all about it, okay?"

I stepped inside and shut the door behind me, and waited until Erica and Parker rounded the corner on the left before I looked at Keegan and broke down. "I'm freaking out! I don't know what to do, I was—I said a lot to Coen to make him think I didn't want to be with him. I know he was hurt, and it killed me, but—oh, God, Keegan . . . I couldn't do it." I took deep breaths in and out and walked into the living room to drop onto the couch. "He'd leave someday. I know he would. And Parker was falling so in love with him. You should see them together! They've barely spent any time together, and already they're so close."

"Reagan—"

"He came over last night, and it was perfect. The three of us, the whole thing, it was perfect," I choked out. My throat felt like it was closing up, but I refused to start crying over this now. I was afraid once I started crying, I wouldn't stop. "But this morning when I woke Parker up, he asked if Coen was going to be his dad."

Keegan's eyes widened and his eyebrows rose. "Uh . . ."

I moved my hands frantically in front of me as I tried to get him to understand the enormity of that. "Two nights together. Two, Keegan. Well, three I guess if you count the dinner when you got out. But that's beside the point. Three nights, and he asked if Coen was going to be his dad. And he sounded like he wanted it, you know?"

"Seriously, Ray—"

"Then, you know what he told me? He told me the next time he saw Coen, he was going to ask if he could *call* him 'Dad.' I know Coen would eventually leave, and I've been protecting Parker and me from that for years . . . but I kept letting myself hope that maybe somehow it would be different because for the first time I actually wanted to be with someone. But after this morning? Well, honestly, it kinda scared the shit out of me how fast all this progressed. But the more I thought about it, the more it felt right for Coen and me. But I knew—I just knew if Parker said that to him it would scare Coen away. And I wouldn't know how to explain to Parker that he wasn't the reason Coen wasn't coming around anymore." I knew I was rambling, but I couldn't stop. I needed to ramble. I needed to freak out to my big brother so I wouldn't lose it while I was alone with Parker later. "I don't know if Parker is old enough to understand all of this yet. God, I feel sick. I hated saying that to Coen. I just don't know, Keegan. But I couldn't risk him running away from us—"

"So instead you pushed me away?"

I shot up off the couch and turned around to see Coen standing in Keegan's kitchen, his face livid.

"Oh God," I whispered, and placed a hand on my sensitive stomach. I was going to throw up . . . or faint. I just couldn't figure out which.

"Instead of letting it all play out . . . instead of letting me *surprise* you, you took all that away from me. You made my decision for me because you were so sure I would leave when I heard that?"

"It hasn't even been two weeks, Coen! Not even two weeks with Parker and he wants you to be his dad. You can't tell me that doesn't freak you out."

He laughed and lifted his hands in the air before letting them drop to his sides. "Well, according to you, that's exactly what it does. It freaks me out and makes me want to run."

"What twenty-four-year-old wants to suddenly become a father to a six-year-old?" I argued, and flung my arm in the direction of the room Parker and Erica were in.

Coen's eyebrows slammed down and his eyes narrowed. "I can't think of many," he said darkly before walking to the back of the couch and resting his hands on the top of it. "But tell me this. What guy goes into a relationship with a single mother and *doesn't* factor her kid into that relationship?"

Crossing my arms, I met his dark stare and laughed humorlessly. "A lot, actually."

"Yeah. A lot of assholes who don't care about the most important thing in their girlfriend's life. And if that's how you view me, then you were right to end this," he said, and waved his hand between us. "Because that means you don't know me at all. Well, apparently you do since you knew without a doubt I would run away from you," he sneered.

"And you're telling me you wouldn't? You're telling me one day you wouldn't leave?" I nearly yelled, and covered my mouth when I realized that I was. Looking back over to Keegan, I realized he wasn't in the room anymore and I wasn't sure if I was glad for that or not.

"I don't know, Reagan. People date, they break up. Others date and get married. Who knows what would've happened between us?"

"That's it!" I flung my hand out toward him before bringing it back to rub at my forehead. "That's exactly it. There is a very real possibility that we would've broken up anyway, and Parker was getting too attached as it was. If I had let our relationship go on, only for it to end months or years down the road . . . it would crush him. This is why I don't let men into our lives."

"No, it's because you're fucking scared!" he yelled, and I jumped back. "I get not wanting to have a bunch of guys coming in and out of his life. I get that, and I think you're right in not wanting that for him. But you're not giving yourself the chance to be with someone, and you're not giving Parker the chance to ever have a dad because the first guy in six years who you'll give the time of day, you push away after only a couple weeks."

"I'm protecting him!" I gritted out.

"Yeah, you're protecting him. There are also people who put their kids in plastic bubbles because they don't want them to get sick. Are you gonna do that too?"

"Do not belittle me for the way I am living and have raised my son!"

The anger slowly left Coen's face, leaving only pain. "You're an amazing mom. There's no questioning that," he said gruffly as he rounded the couch and walked toward me until he had me backed up against a wall. "But you're scared of getting hurt, and you're terrified Parker will get hurt as the result. I get it. I swear to God I get it."

I shook my head and tried to steady my quivering jaw. He couldn't understand. No one—unless they were in my situation—could understand.

"You're right, Reagan. Actually being a father hasn't crossed my mind. And, no, I don't know how I would have reacted if Parker had asked me if he could call me that; but I know it wouldn't have made me bolt for the door. Because I knew he came with you. And you? God, woman, you fucking know how to piss me off . . . but that doesn't stop me from wanting you so damn bad. But I do know this. I know that your son is the coolest fucking kid I've ever met. I know that last night was the best night of my life. The *whole* night, not just after Parker went to bed. I know that I want a lot more nights just like it. And I know that what *did* freak me out, was the thought of not having it again when you were telling me it was over this morning."

"Coen . . ." I swallowed roughly and looked away when his thumb brushed against my jaw. "I'm trying to save all of us a lot of hurt down the road. This can't work between us."

"How do you figure? Because last night and this morning, I could've sworn you were thinking the opposite."

My cheeks heated and I tried to push away the memories that kept assaulting me from our time together. "Almost all of our conversations begin with arguments. Have you realized that?"

"Yeah," he said without missing a beat. "And how have all of those arguments ended? Just like this one. With you in my arms, and with you fighting what you want."

"That's not something to be proud of, Coen. It can't be healthy for people in a relationship to have most their conversations start as fights. What if Parker starts catching on to that? And I don't willingly go into your arms, you always back me up against something so I don't have any other option!"

Coen just smiled and shook his head once as he

got somehow, impossibly, closer to me. "We argue because you're a bitch and I'm a dick, and neither of us know how to keep our mouths shut. We argue because you're usually fighting me on something, or trying to protect yourself and Parker, and I'm trying to get you to see how ridiculous you're being. We argue because that's *our* way of talking through things. We get loud, yeah, but we don't scream at each other, we don't throw shit, and you will never in your life see me raising a hand to you or any woman. So we argue? Who fucking cares, Reagan? At least we don't have to worry about our first fight. At least we don't have to worry about communication issues. This is how we talk, and when we've talked everything out, we're fine."

"Always the charmer, Coen. You really think you can call me a bitch, and I'll just swoon or something because you tried to justify it?"

He looked at me for a few seconds before whispering, "Yeah, Duchess, I do."

"That's not how—" My words cut off on a high-pitched whimper when his mouth pressing firmly against mine, and it took a few seconds of giving into his kiss before I pushed him back. "No, I'm not done being mad!"

Coen's dark eyes held mine, the humor now gone. "You're not mad at me, Reagan. You're trying to protect yourself again, and in doing that you've tried to find reasons to be pissed. If anyone should be mad here, it's me. You tried to take you and Parker from me because *you* thought I would run. You tried to take away my say in *our* relationship. If I really thought you wanted to break up, then this wouldn't be happening. But I know what you're trying to do, and I'm not going to let you."

"I'm—"

"Scared. You're scared, baby, I know."

My jaw trembled harder and tears pricked at the back of my eyes.

"We can have this argument a thousand more times than we already have, Duchess, and I'm still going to be here, fighting for our chance. What Parker said scared *you* today. Not me. You. But like I said, I know you don't want to break up. I know you want this just as bad as I do. We can go back a few steps, we can slow things down. I won't come over, I won't stay the night . . . whatever it takes for you not to be scared."

"We can't, Coen, that's just it. Did you not hear what I said to Keegan? Everything's fast with us, but fast feels right when I'm with you. I just—" I cut off on a strained sob and dropped my face into my hands. "This isn't some insecurity of mine that you will leave me. This isn't me being ridiculous because I don't want to lose you. I can't have Parker lose you, do you understand? I can't have him fall in love with you and lose you! It seems dumb to you, it may seem dumb to everyone . . . but *his* heart is my priority . . . not mine."

Coen moved my hands from my face, and tilted my head back so he could brush the tears back. He stayed silent for long minutes as he cradled my face in his hands, and I braced myself for when he would finally agree with me. Agree that he couldn't do this.

"I can't promise a future, Reagan," he began softly. "I can't promise a future because I've seen too many lives cut short. Nothing is certain. But with what you know about me, with how I feel about you; you can be assured that leaving you—leaving the woman who silences my demons—is the last thing I want. You asked me why I pushed so hard for this . . . do you not see me still fighting for us? Fighting after only a couple weeks for something that neither of us can guarantee?"

Blinking away more tears, I looked up into his pained expression, and everything in me ached at the hurt I saw there.

"You're terrified of what will happen to you and Parker if I leave . . . have you even realized that you already gave me a taste of what it would be like for *you* to leave?"

"Coen," I cried out, and covered my mouth with shaky hands.

"I can't promise you forever. But neither can you. All I can promise you is that I want you, I want to be with you, I want to be there for your son—and I can't begin to fathom hurting either of you." His dark eyes moved back and forth between mine for a few seconds. "Okay?"

I nodded and managed to choke out, " 'Kay."

A soft breath blew past his lips as relief settled over his face. "Now can we stop with this bullshit? I told you, I'll have this same fight with you a thousand times, but Duchess, that doesn't mean it *shouldn't* stop. There has to be some kind of trust between us. Agreed?"

"Agreed," I whispered.

Brushing a kiss across my lips, he wiped my cheeks with his thumbs once more before letting his forehead fall against mine and releasing a heavy sigh. "Jesus Christ, Duchess. I told you, you'll be the death of me," he said softly, before stepping back and bringing me away from the wall.

Walking us back toward the couch, he pulled me down so I was sitting sideways on his lap and wrapped his arms around me. "I'm sorry."

His hand paused for a second before continuing on the path up and down my back. "I know you are. But we fought it out, talked everything through, and it's behind us now. So there's no need to say you're sorry anymore."

I couldn't even remember if I'd said sorry before, and I needed to apologize for everything I'd done. I looked up at him, and waited for his dark eyes to meet mine. "I'm not sure if I agree with—"

"Parker, wait!" I heard Erica say just before I heard my son's voice. "Coen!"

Coen easily slid me off his lap, a large smile replacing the worn-out mask from our fight. "Hey, bud!"

"Are you going to be my dad?" Parker jumped up on the couch on the other side of Coen and waited expectantly for an answer.

Even though Coen knew this was probably coming,

even though we'd just talked—er, fought—about this, my body still tensed at what Coen's reaction would be.

Coen seemed to think really hard for Parker's benefit before shrugging slowly. "I don't know, bud. Your mom and I still have a long ways to go before we'll know that."

Parker's face scrunched together, and I knew he didn't understand why Coen didn't have a definite answer right now.

"But I promise you this: You'll be the first one to know if I get to become your dad. Deal?" Coen asked, holding out his hand.

Parker slapped his hand against Coen's and smiled widely at him. "Deal!"

Get to . . . he said get *to become your dad.* My heart warmed and somehow seemed to ache even more when I realized I'd almost taken this away from all of us. Again.

When Parker took off for the kitchen, Coen leaned toward me and pulled my legs over his lap again. "Jesus. Thank God you warned me about that. If I would've gone into that blind, I might have taken off." Coen blew out a heavy breath before giving me a teasing grin.

I slapped his stomach and narrowed my eyes at him. "You just ruined this perfect illusion I was having of you."

He smiled warmly and pulled me closer to place kisses behind my ear. "Then we're right where we should be, Duchess, because I'm nowhere near perfect."

Chapter Eight

Coen—*September 16, 2010*

A GUTTURAL YELL tore through my throat as I flew up into a sitting position and looked wildly around me. My breaths were coming too fast, and it took my mind too long to comprehend that I was once again here. My condo. Where I was every morning I wasn't at Reagan's.

But everything had once again felt too real. I could feel the dry heat, hear the tortured screams, smell the rust, human waste, and gunpowder, see the—

I pushed the heels of my palms against my eyes, and let out an agonized breath.

Standing from the couch I'd fallen asleep on sometime late this morning, I pulled my sweat-soaked clothes off my body and threw them in the hamper as I walked toward the bathroom. Turning the water on as hot as it would go, I paced anxiously as I waited for the room to begin steaming up before standing under the scorching spray. I gritted my teeth against the initial sting, but soon my body began relaxing under the relentless pelting, and I rested my hands against the wall, letting my head hang as I tried to forget.

Some of the men on base told me it was best to let go. Let go? I couldn't fucking let go. They were gone. My men were gone . . . and I hadn't saved them. I'd had to see their wives, their children, and their families when I'd returned. I'd had to look one of their very pregnant wives in the face and tell her I hadn't been able to keep my promise in bringing her husband back.

There was no letting that shit go. Not when the only reason I was here, instead of in the ground with them, was because I'd fallen into a trap—which triggered the ambush—and was knocked unconscious while they were all captured. I should have been paying better attention. I should have seen it coming. And I hadn't.

Yeah . . . there was no way to "let go."

Stepping out of the shower, I grabbed a towel and was drying my skin when I heard my phone go off in the other room. Moving quickly toward it, I frowned when I saw the name on the screen. I swear, it was like he knew now was not the time to talk.

But for some reason, I still answered.

"Yeah?"

"Steele! How've you been?"

I sat down on the couch and bit back a sigh. "Good. What's new in the Saco house?"

There was silence for a few moments before he said, "Did you have a nightmare?"

I finally released the sigh and sat back on the couch, running my hand over my face. "I asked what's new in the Saco house."

"And I asked if you had a fucking nightmare."

"Of course I had fucking flashbacks, I have to sleep at some point!"

"Steele . . . man, you've got to talk to someone."

"Don't need to. They won't understand. All they'll do is piss me off because they'll act like they know how I feel. They'll act like they know what I went through. And why? Because they have a goddamn degree? Fuck that. No, I'm not talking to anyone."

"You can't do this to yourself. You can't live like this. I thought—I thought you said it was getting better."

I stared blankly at the ceiling and shrugged even though he couldn't see me. "It is." He didn't respond, and I didn't expand on that for a few moments. "It's her, Saco. I don't know what it is about her. But when I'm around her, it's all gone. There's nothing. No missions. No men left behind. No—" I cut off and ground my jaw.

I'd told Saco all about Reagan and Parker, and the struggles I'd gone through just to get Reagan to give us a chance. I just hadn't told him that she also made all the bullshit disappear, because at the time there hadn't been a reason to.

"Nothing," he said suspiciously.

"Nothing," I confirmed. "And when I sleep with her, I actually sleep. For hours . . . uninterrupted, no flashbacks, nothing. Reagan and Parker are my peace," I mumbled the words I'd told Reagan almost a month ago, not at all worried about Saco judging me for them. He knew what this meant for me.

"And does she know about this?"

"She knows what she can."

Saco was quiet for a long time before he finally huffed a short laugh. "Does she have any idea what she means to you?"

"Not a clue. But I'm trying to show her."

"Good, man. I'm happy for you. I bet Hudson is too."

I raised an eyebrow. "I don't know about that. I mean, he is, but I've already been punched once."

Saco laughed loudly and I rolled my eyes.

"Keep laughing, asshole."

"Why'd he punch you?"

"He walked into her apartment when we were on the couch. She was riding me. Fucking bastard needs to learn how to call before he just shows up."

Saco just laughed louder.

"So tell me what's going on in Oregon. How's your son?"

"Tate's great, man. I wish you could see him. Little man looks just like me."

"Ugly as shit?"

"Fuck you, Steele," he teased, but there was no

doubting the pride in his voice. "You guys really do need to get over here though. Maybe I can convince you and Hudson to come out for his first birthday in May or something."

"Aw, do we get to be his uncles? I'm touched, Saco, really I am." There was a long silence as we tried to avoid what we both knew came next. "And Olivia?"

There was a weighted sigh on the other end of the call, and I knew things with his wife were just as bad as they'd always been. They'd only been together for the sake of having someone to fuck when she'd gotten pregnant and he'd married her. Something all of us, and his family, had tried to stop him from, but he wanted to do the right thing.

"Liv's being Liv. She spends most of her time with her parents. We only really talk because of Tate, but she's barely around him. Only to feed him and dress him, because apparently I don't know how to dress a child. Other than that, he's with me all day unless he's sleeping. So, I don't know. It's awkward. Like, we both know we can't stand each other, but don't say anything."

"I'm sorry, man."

"Don't say it," he warned.

My eyebrows pinched together. "What?"

"Don't tell me you told me so. I did what I thought was right for Olivia. She shouldn't have had to go through that alone . . . and now I know I did the right thing for Tate. He needs two parents."

"I wasn't going to. I said what I had to say before you married her, and when she wouldn't let you see your son. But I'm not going to sit here and tell you what I think of your decisions every time we talk. You did what you had to. End of story."

"Yeah," he said softly, and then cursed. "Tate's up. I gotta go."

"All right, man. I'll talk to you soon."

"Sounds good. And Steele? Just because Reagan gives you some relief, doesn't mean you have to suffer the rest of the time. You can't live like this. You *need* to talk to someone, please think about it. You have—you have to start moving on."

"Start moving on? Are you shitting me?"

"No, I—"

"You saw what I'd been in for those hours before you rescued me. You only saw the aftermath, you didn't watch it happen to them. You weren't forced to watch every fucking second of it. You didn't feel like a worthless piece of shit who did *nothing*—"

"You couldn't, Steele," he said, cutting me off. "When will you realize that? You couldn't do anything. Just like the others weren't able to do anything when the rest were killed. It could have just as easily been you. I'm sorry you were forced to watch that. Steele . . . I'm so goddamn sorry we didn't get there earlier. But I couldn't spend my life being tortured by what happened, knowing that my team was too late to save the rest of yours. So don't let your life slip by while you're being tortured by something you had no control over. Get some help."

I let the phone fall onto the couch beside me when

he ended the call, and leaned forward to hold my head in my hands. If only it were that easy.

Reagan—*September 17, 2010*

"HEY THERE, STRANGER," I called out as I shut the door behind me to Coen's studio and ran into his waiting arms.

"Good morning, Duchess. How'd you sleep?"

I pressed my lips to his chest and pulled away, but kept my hand firmly in his. "Not nearly as good as I do when you're there, but pretty well. You?"

Coen's eyes flashed to one of the couches, and his face fell for a second before he laughed awkwardly. "Uh, I'm pretty sure I got about twenty minutes in there somewhere."

I stared at his dark eyes for a long time, looking for any signs that he hadn't slept . . . but he could go without sleep for days, and I'd probably never know. He hid things that well. But with Keegan's odd question about Coen sleeping, and then the first night Coen had spent the night and had seemed to be in awe over the fact that he'd slept . . . I wouldn't put it past Coen to be telling me the truth.

Deciding not to breach that subject right now, I looked at his laptop and my eyes widened. "Oh my God. Coen, is this one of your shoots?"

"Uh, yeah . . . I guess we haven't really talked about this yet."

I shot him a confused look before stepping closer to the laptop. "Can I look through them?"

His dark eyes widened and he shrugged before reaching for a coffee cup. "If you want. I just finished editing those before you got here."

Sitting down at the desk, I clicked through a shoot of a tattooed girl on a couch in nothing but a lacy pair of underwear. Her arms had been perfectly positioned to cover her bare breasts in the different positions. It was beautiful and seductive, and I'd frowned by the time I got to the last one.

"Are there more shoots?"

Coen was staring at me like he was waiting for something.

"Do you not want me to look at these?"

He kept looking at me before flashing his eyes at the screen. "I'm waiting for you to get mad."

"Why would I get mad?"

Nodding in the direction of the laptop, he kept his eyes pinned on mine. "She was topless. She only had underwear on. This was a week and a half ago. I'm just waiting for you to react like a normal girlfriend."

My lips twitched. "And how would a normal girlfriend react?"

He put the hand holding the coffee cup out in front of him and raised his shoulders up. "I don't know. Yell. Say you don't want me doing those kinds of shoots. Be jealous, I don't know."

I widened my eyes and acted like I was really considering doing just that. "Well, we both know how much I love to argue with you. But that"—I gestured toward the screen—"is amazing. Besides, Keegan already told me you did those kinds of photos sometimes. It's not like it was a secret."

"Of course it wasn't a secret, Reagan. But it's one thing to know about it, its another to see it."

I smiled softly at him. "Does it *bother* me? I would be lying if I said it didn't. Do I think what you did with that shoot was beautiful? Absolutely. Do I wish I had her body? Hell yes." Coen made a face, but I kept going. "Would I ever ask you to stop doing those shoots? No."

"Where did you come from?" he muttered.

"The way I see it, you were doing these long before we started seeing each other. So I know that if there *was* something to be worried about with these shoots, then it would have been going on even back then, and we would have never started dating."

Coen stared at me in awe for a few seconds without saying anything. Just before I asked if he was okay, he asked, "Can I pull a Parker?"

"A Parker?"

"You, Duchess, are the *coolest*."

I laughed loudly before turning back around in the chair to face the laptop. "Can I see more?"

He stepped up behind me and kissed the top of my head as he clicked through his files to where all his shoots were. "Knock yourself out. If you don't want to stay through the whole shoot, I'll call you when I'm done, all right?"

I nodded and tilted my head to the side when he brushed his lips against my neck, and shamelessly watched as he set up his studio. But by the time his client got there, I'd barely spared the guy a glance before getting caught up in the thousands upon thousands of pictures on Coen's laptop.

There were some more like the first one I'd looked through. Some couple shots and weddings. The ones of the guy when I'd first come to the studio, and a lot of this guy I was having trouble figuring out if he was a firefighter, model, or fitness athlete. Then there were the more artistic ones, where every new set had me leaning closer to the laptop, and falling more in love with Coen's style.

Clicking on the last file, labeled "bullshit," my eyebrows rose and eyes darted to Coen before quickly going back to the screen. My mouth slowly fell open as I clicked through picture after picture of Coen. It was at probably the twelfth photo that my eyebrows dropped and pinched together, before I rapidly clicked back to the beginning and started over again, this time going through faster.

Sitting back in the chair, I folded my arms over my chest and angled my head to the side as I stared at the picture of him filling the screen. I don't know how many pictures I'd finally gone through of him before stopping. Close to one hundred? Every one of them had been amazing, or funny, or artsy, or just sexy as sin. But that's not why I couldn't go through any more. I couldn't go through any more because in every single picture, Coen's face was somehow covered. Either by a shadow, glasses, mask, hat, cameras, paint . . . something. There wasn't one that was just him.

"I didn't think you'd sta—find the lame folder."

Looking up at him, I pointed to the screen. "Do you have an issue with your face?"

He looked at me like I was losing it before laughing awkwardly. "Uh. What?"

"Your face"—sitting back up, I pushed down the left arrow and let it flip through the pictures—"is covered in every single one of these pictures. Why?"

"I don't know, I like being weird? Or going for that artsy shit."

"You sure that's it?"

Coen shook his head slowly, like he didn't know what other answer I could possibly be expecting. "I'm pretty sure. I mean, you've seen my face. If I had an issue with it, I wouldn't let you see it."

"Exactly," I whispered when I looked back at the screen.

"I don't know what you're getting at, babe."

I took a deep breath in before looking at him. "All those pictures—and there's a lot of them—were taken in the last couple years."

"Yeah . . . ?"

"Whatever happened for you to have your demons, when did it happen?"

Coen straightened and continued to stare at me without responding.

"Was it before—"

"There were missions throughout the last five years, it's from all of them."

"The main thing," I pressed. "There has to be something crucial that happened. I don't doubt there was bad shit every time you were sent somewhere. But I also don't doubt there was something huge that is tormenting you." When I realized he wasn't going to answer, and that I'd probably asked way too much of him, I clicked out of the pictures and curled in on myself. "I'm sorry, I shouldn't have—"

"Two and a half years ago."

I looked up into his haunted eyes, and ached to help him somehow.

"It was two and a half years ago. About four or five months before any of those pictures of me. I, uh, deleted all the pictures of me from before that time."

I just nodded when his eyes focused back on me. That's what I'd been worried about. Not that the pictures of him weren't incredible, but somehow, I'd known. Coen was always, even subconsciously, hiding the place where his demons resided.

"Come here," Coen said suddenly.

I shot him a look but gave him my hand to pull me up.

"Follow me."

"Okay . . ." The word trailed off as Coen pulled his shirt over his head, and continued walking toward where all the equipment was set up.

Flipping off a few things, and switching others on,

he moved his camera and played with it for a while before coming back over to me.

"You ready?"

"Um, I'm actually kind of lost right now. You took off your shirt and I started staring, and then you were playing with everything . . ."

He grinned before grabbing the bottom of my shirt, and slowly pulled it off my body.

"What are you—"

"I'm showing my girlfriend that she's more beautiful than any of the girls she saw in those photos. I'm about to do my first shoot *with* someone. And if anything will be covering my face, it will be some part of you." Unclasping my bra, he slid the straps down my arms before letting it drop to the floor.

"Coen," I said breathlessly, my lips pulling into a grin. I knew he was distracting me, I knew he was distracting himself . . . but I didn't care. I loved that he was doing this.

"And, besides, that bed and couch are both new. I knew if I ever wanted you on anything in this studio, I didn't want it to have been touched before or to have any memories tied to it. They were delivered yesterday . . . so I think we should break them in, what about you?"

I smiled and leaned up to capture his bottom lip between my teeth. "My parents can't see these pictures."

He laughed. "Or your brother."

We started standing. Both keeping only our jeans

on as we posed chest to chest, his chest to my back
with his tattooed arms covering my breasts, and me
behind him—clinging to his body. Then he moved me
so my back was against the wall, legs around his hips,
chests flush as he tortured my lips with teasing bites.

By the time he released my legs, and began unbuttoning my jeans, I'd forgotten we were doing this in
front of his camera.

He finished pulling my jeans off before walking us
toward the large bed and getting us both on top of
it. Holding his body over mine, I ran my hands over
the hard muscles in his arms and hiked one bare leg
up around his hip. It wasn't until the flash that I realized why he'd been slowly moving my arm until it
was covering my exposed breasts, or why he'd continued nudging my head back with his nose to hang off
the side of the bed. Through this slow-building, erotic
type of foreplay we'd started on, he was still positioning us, still making sure I was somehow covered, and,
I'm sure, still making it all look effortless.

Because with him, it was.

And it was soon after, when he pulled off my
underwear, and allowed me to rid him of his jeans
and boxer briefs as he tossed aside the remote for the
camera, that I realized I was no longer okay with not
having a forever with Coen Steele. As he slowly made
love to me on that bed, I knew that I'd fallen in love
with him, and anything less than forever wouldn't be
enough.

Chapter Nine

Coen—*September 25, 2010*

KNOCKING QUICKLY ON Reagan's door, I glanced at my car and blew out a quick breath before facing the door again right before it was flung open.

"Coen!"

"What's up, bud?" Grabbing under Parker's arms, I lifted him into a hug before throwing him over my shoulder.

He laughed wildly and slapped on my back. "Hey, I thought you weren't strong!"

"I'm not." I gasped, and stopped walking. Letting my legs shake a little, I acted like my knees were buckling under his weight. "You're too heavy for me."

"No, I'm not!" he squealed.

"Either we're both going down, or just you."

"Both!"

Letting him slide forward on my shoulder a little bit, I gasped and pretended to struggle. "I can't keep you up—I can't." Sliding him the rest of the way off, I swung him down, acting like I just barely caught him before his head hit the floor.

His laughter filled the entire apartment before he lifted his head and slapped on my forearms. "Do it again."

I widened my eyes, and let my face fall. "I can't . . . you're still . . . too . . . heavy," I grunted out each word as I let him slip down onto the carpet an inch at a time. Once he was on the floor, I doubled over, breathing heavily.

Parker jumped up and tackled me onto the ground. "You're weak, Coen, you shoulda eaten your food growing up."

I smiled over at him. "Shoulda. How was school yesterday?"

"It was cool."

"You and Jason still best friends?"

"Yep."

"Girls still have cooties?"

Parker's eyes widened, and he stopped where he'd been tracing one of the stars on my forearm. "Yeah," he said softly. Like I should have known his answer wouldn't have changed in a day. But with six-year-olds, you never knew. He and Jason decided they hated each other and were back to best friends twice in one day.

Holding up my fist for him to bump, I ruffled his

hair and stood up. "Sounds like your world is still pretty perfect then, bud. Come on, let's go see what's taking your mom—" I cut off and froze when I saw Reagan standing there. She looked beautiful. Clearing my throat, I licked my lips and finished my sentence. "So long."

Raising an eyebrow, an amused smirk tugged at her full lips before she pushed off the wall to walk toward us. "Take *me* so long, huh? I've been ready."

Pulling her into my arms, I pressed a kiss to her forehead. "You look beautiful."

Her smirk widened into a smile. "Thank you, are you going to tell me what we're doing today?"

"Are you going to tell me how long you were standing there?"

"Long enough."

I considered her answer and narrowed my eyes at her. "Yeah, still not telling you where we're going. But we need to go."

"Fine, fine. Parker, you ready?" she asked as she pulled away from me.

When she grabbed her purse and keys, I rubbed at the back of my neck and sucked in a deep breath. "Can I drive?" I asked, and I'm pretty sure I held my breath as I waited for her answer.

Her brow furrowed. "You want to drive my car?"

"No, uh . . . can I drive us in my car?"

"Um, yeah, I guess. We just have to move the booster seat first."

"I kinda bought one," I said tightly. It felt like I broke

out in a cold sweat as I waited for her to freak out. To say this was moving too fast. For us to have the argument we'd somehow avoided for a couple weeks, again.

Reagan's eyes widened and mouth opened slowly. "You bought a booster seat for your car?" she asked softly.

"Yeah, but if it bothers you—"

I don't know what happened first, it seemed to all happen at once. Her purse and keys dropped to the floor, her hazel eyes filled with tears, and she launched her small body at me—wrapping her arms tightly around my waist.

"You didn't have to do that," she said against my chest.

"Actually, I did." Running my hand over her long hair, I waited until she looked up at me again. "I couldn't drive you two anywhere unless we moved *your* booster seat. It was stupid. I need to be able to drive him without having to inconvenience you. This was necessary for us."

Her head shook slowly back and forth, and she huffed softly. "I—" She cut off quickly and cleared her throat. "Thank you. You have no idea how much this means to me."

Pushing back the hair from her face, I cupped her cheek and kissed her slowly. "I think I have an idea."

There was a loud, exaggerated sigh next to us. "Are we *going*?"

Reagan and I both laughed and looked at Parker. "Yeah, bud, let's go." Grabbing Reagan's purse and keys, I handed them back to her and led them out the door. As we walked to my car, I nudged her shoulder. "Hey, Duchess."

"Hmm?"

Hooking my arm around her neck, I pressed my lips close to her ear and whispered, "Do you realize you took my compliment back there? Pretty sure that's a first."

Her face scrunched together as she thought for a moment before she rolled her eyes, scoffed, and pushed me away. "And I'm pretty sure you're still delusional."

Looking at my girl as she put Parker in the back seat of my car, I shook my head. "No. Definitely not that."

"WE'RE GOING TO the park?" Reagan asked a few minutes later. "Why'd you have us dress nice if we were going here?"

I bit back a smile and turned to go around to a different side. "You'll see."

"Are we gonna play?" Coen asked from the backseat.

"Not today, bud. I have something else in mind. But when we're done, I'll take you wherever you want for lunch. How's that sound?"

"Cool!"

I smiled over at Reagan, and we both mouthed, "Cool."

"I don't think I've been to this side," she mumbled, and grabbed the ends of her hair.

Grabbing for her hands, I pulled them away and wrapped my fingers securely around them. "So . . . our impromptu shoot last week gave me an idea." Glancing at her, I watched as her cheeks stained with heat.

"W-what, uh, what kind of idea?" she stammered.

As soon as I stopped the car, I pointed out her window. "It's over there."

Her brow scrunched together for a few seconds. "Is that . . . ?"

"My equipment? Yeah."

She turned quickly, her face lit up with excitement. "You're going to shoot us?"

"You're going to shoot us?" Parker asked loudly, horror lacing his tone.

I barked a laugh before I could compose myself. "No way, bud. Not like that. I'm going to take pictures of you and your mom. Its called a photo *shoot*, that's the kind of shoot she meant."

A relieved look crossed his face. "Oh. Cool."

Looking back at Reagan, I leaned close. "Is that okay?"

"More than okay." Taking off her seat belt, she opened her door and stepped out before leaning back in. "I do love when you surprise me, Coen Steele."

I just plain loved her.

Getting out of the car, I pulled my camera out of the trunk, and walked over to where Reagan and Parker were waiting for me. "Ready?"

Parker grabbed my hand and nodded hard once. "Ready!"

My chest tightened and I looked at Parker before looking up at Reagan. A soft smile was slowly covering her face as her eyes stayed glued to our hands, and just before she began walking, her hazel eyes met mine and I knew she was feeling this too. She loved me, I had no doubt of that. But it wasn't just the two of us, my love went so much deeper than just Reagan. I loved her son, and I loved the three of us together. And from the look she'd just given me, I knew she felt the same.

We walked up to the hill I'd had two of my friends set up my equipment on, and after introducing them to Reagan and Parker, we got started. Parker wasn't into it at first because he was still afraid someone was going to *shoot* him, so after having one of my buddies take pictures of Parker and me flexing, and fighting with imaginary light sabers, then a few of Reagan and me together, he was more than ready for his turn to take pictures with his mom—which he let us know by jumping into the pictures of us.

And as I stared at the two of them from behind the lens of my camera, a feeling unlike anything I'd ever experienced washed over me. It was calming, freeing, and I knew I would do anything to make it last. Parker laughed loudly at something Reagan said to him as I changed the setting on my camera, and the sound filled me—making me smile. I quickly captured the moment before it could end, and finally realized what the feeling was.

Peace.

Reagan—*October 1, 2010*

CRACKING MY EYES open, I frowned when I saw what time it was. I had thirty minutes before I had to get Parker up and ready for school. Which meant twenty-nine minutes before the warm body wrapped around mine would leave. At least it was the first Friday of the month, which meant we would be spending the day together . . . but I hated watching him leave in the mornings.

Rolling over, I curled up against his bare chest and placed soft kisses there as I let my free hand lightly trail up his back. Goose bumps covered his skin, and I smiled before moving up to his throat and jaw.

His chest rumbled. "Duchess."

"Morning," I said softly, and waited for what I knew would come next.

"Time?"

"Six."

Coen breathed in deeply through his nose, and a smile crossed his face. "Amazing," he murmured, and tightened his arms around me.

"Tell me why?"

His eyes barely opened, and he didn't speak, but the question was clear on his face.

"You're sleeping here about three times a week, and each time you just can't seem to believe that it's morning when we wake up. You're always in awe, why is that?"

Dark eyes now fully on me, his face remained blank.

I moved so I was lying on my stomach, and played with the sheet below me, studying it intently. "Keegan said something at the very beginning of us seeing each other."

"And what was that?" he asked, his tone dark—and I knew then, whatever this was had to do with whatever was haunting him.

"He asked if you slept. But at the time we hadn't slept together, so he dropped the subject." Risking a glance at him, I asked softly, "Do you not sleep?"

Coen studied me for a long time before releasing a harsh breath. "Not if I'm not with you. I mean—I do. But I don't like to. Some nights I don't sleep at all, others I get an hour and a half to two hours . . . and that's if I'm not able to wake myself up after thirty minutes."

"Thirty . . . what? Why thirty?"

Rolling onto his back, he stared blankly at the ceiling and rested his hands on his chest. "I have flashbacks if I sleep."

"From whatever happened two and a half years ago?"

"Mostly. Sometimes other missions."

I watched the haunted look fall over his face and pressed my palm to his cheek, turning his head so he was looking at me. A calmness slowly filled his features, and he grabbed my hand to kiss it.

"Why do you sleep with me, do you think?"

He shrugged. "I have no idea. That first night here, I hadn't planned on actually falling asleep, next thing I knew it was six hours later and you were waking me up."

"And you've never had a nightmare—"

"Flashback."

"You've never had a flashback when you sleep with me?"

His dark eyes held mine as he shook his head.

"Have you—have you thought about talking to someone?"

Coen sighed and sat up, but his face showed all the patience in the world as he pulled me into his chest. "I'm not going to talk to anyone. Your brother and Saco try to get me to all the time. And before you ask why, it's because even though those people are trained to help . . . they couldn't possibly understand because they've never gone through anything like what we went through."

"Okay, I get that. But you're not sleeping," I argued softly, and gripped the back of his neck as I sat up to rest my forehead against his. "That alone can cause depression, and if you're already dealing with . . . whatever it is you're dealing with—"

A laugh rumbled in Coen's chest. "Do I seem depressed to you, Ray?"

I didn't find anything about this amusing. I was terrified for him. "You worry me sometimes," I replied honestly.

His dark eyes widened, and surprise covered his features. "What?"

"Sometimes the things you say . . . they're dark. Your words are haunted, and they show just how haunted you are up here." I touched his temple with the tips of my fingers. "But I know you went through things no one should have to, so I understand you. That doesn't mean I'm not worried. And then the pictures you take of yourself. I love them, Coen, I do. They're . . . different, edgy, sexy, some are hilarious. But you and I both know why you hide your face or your eyes, even if you're not meaning to."

Coen was quiet for so long, I started to think I'd pushed him too far. Sitting back on his lap, I looked at his tortured face, and my heart broke.

"That's what I do."

"What?"

Looking up at me, he repeated, "That's what I do. When I can't sleep, or when I'm avoiding it, I edit pictures, or go do shoots of myself. It gives me something to think about other than what I feel like I'm running from."

Letting my hands run over his shoulders, I looked at the path they were making as the tension left Coen's body. "I wish I could take it away for you."

He laughed sadly. "I already told you, you do. I don't know why, and I don't know how . . . but you do."

Pressing a kiss to his lips, I sat back and eyed him for a second. "I won't bring up talking to someone

again. I get why you don't want to, even though
I wish you would. But, maybe . . . maybe someday
you'll tell me." His face hardened, and I hurried to
continue. "Not about the mission—I know you can't
do that—but about what happened. You don't have
to today; you don't have to *ever*. But, Coen, if I chase
your demons away . . . if you can sleep when you're
with me . . . maybe just talking to me will help. I won't
judge you, I won't try to fix you, I just want to be there
for you."

Pushing us until I was on my back and he was hov-
ering over me, he shook his head in wonder. "Again,
where did you come from?"

I placed my hands back on his neck and searched
his face. "I've been right here, waiting for you to come
crashing into our lives."

A slow smile spread across his face. "Reagan . . .
I love you."

My mouth opened, and it felt like my body was
being pricked by millions of needles that were either
ice cold or scorching hot. I couldn't figure out which.
My heart began racing, and I was trying to figure out
if I'd imagined those words that were replaying them-
selves over and over again. "You—"

"Love you," he finished for me.

My mouth stretched into a wide grin seconds
before I brought his face to mine. "I love you too," I
breathed against his lips, and kissed him again.

His tongue brushed against mine and I whimpered
into his mouth when he pulled my body off the bed.

Wrapping his arms tightly around my waist, he deepened the kiss for a few more moments before pulling back and placing a gentle kiss on the end of my nose.

"Maybe someday I'll be able to tell you what happened. For now, this is all I need."

"Okay." I sighed contentedly. Turning my head to look at the clock, I frowned. I wasn't ready for this time to end, even if only for a couple hours.

Coen's face held the same displeasure I felt. "Do I get to see you today? Or do you have things you have to get done?"

Grabbing the ends of my hair, I nervously played with them and bit down on my cheek as I thought for a second. "What if you didn't leave?"

Coen's fingers went under my chin to lift my head until we were staring at each other. "What do you mean?"

"I mean what if you were here when I woke up Parker, and while he got ready—"

His dark eyes widened. "Can I take him to school?"

His question shocked me, and my head jerked back. I'd been worried he still wasn't ready for Parker to know he stayed the night; I definitely hadn't been prepared for that. "You—you want to take him to school?"

"Well, I mean, you would come with us. But, if it's okay, I'd like to."

"It's okay," I said softly.

"I'll take you to get coffee after, and then we can do whatever you want for the rest of the day."

I raised my eyebrows at him. "Whatever *I* want? Why do I feel like you're trying to bribe me into getting *your* way?"

"Because I want nothing more than to come back here and spend the day in this bed with you. Is it working?"

I smiled wryly at him and crawled off his lap. "Oh yeah. Keep it up, Steele. Now put some clothes on, I have to wake up Parker."

Grabbing my pajama pants and tight V-neck I'd been wearing before Coen had torn them off last night, I slipped them back on and watched as he searched for his clothes. Watching him walk around my bedroom was enough of a distraction for what was about to happen, and I so needed the distraction.

Parker hadn't mentioned the whole dad thing to Coen since that first day nearly a month ago, and Coen and I hadn't talked about it again. I was ready for this—ready for Coen to not have to rush out in the mornings he stayed over, and ready for Parker to start getting used to the idea. But being the first time, I was still scared. Parker could think this meant Coen was going to be his dad, he might not handle it well . . . so many things could happen.

"Ready to see how he handles this?"

I laughed at Coen's worried expression, glad I wasn't the only one freaking out about this. "Ready."

Walking out of my room and down the hall, I opened Parker's door and stepped in. Coen stopped just on the inside of the door frame and leaned up against it, and I was glad he'd been the one to make that decision. Because I couldn't figure out if he should be out in the kitchen, in here with me, or hiding in my bedroom for the next couple hours.

Sitting down on the bed, I rubbed my hand over Parker's back and crooned, "Wake up, buddy. Parker. Wake up."

He rolled over so he was facing me and rubbed at his face.

"Hi, honey."

"Morning, Mom." Looking over, he waved. "Morning, Coen."

"Morning, bud," Coen's deep voice trickled into the room, and something about this scene felt so right to me that I had to sit there trying to swallow past the tightness in my throat before I could speak again.

"Time to get up and get ready for school, okay?"

Rolling out of bed, he shuffled over to Coen and grabbed his hand as he tried to pull him out of the room. "I want cereal, please."

Coen looked over at me and smiled before allowing Parker to pull him into the hall. His voice trailing off as he said, "Whatever you want."

I just sat there as I tried to comprehend what had happened. It had been incredibly anticlimactic for how nervous Coen and I had been, but it had also been beyond perfect. With a smile on my face, I stood and walked out of Parker's room to join them in the kitchen, where Coen was getting Parker's breakfast.

Chapter Ten

Reagan—*October 27, 2010*

I FLASHED A grateful smile at the secretary as she came in to hand me a stack of papers, and continued talking to one of our bigger clients.

"I just sent it over to you; let me know what you think."

As I waited for his response, I flipped quickly through the requests before putting them in the inbox.

"Now, it's a little different from the style you usually go for, but I really think—"

"Love it!"

I smiled and tried to contain the relief in my voice. "I'm glad."

"I love this modern twist you put on it."

"All right, well, make sure it all looks good, and if it does, I'll put the order in."

"No changes, I'm happy with this one, whoever had the balls to change it up on me deserves a raise."

Smiling to myself, I wished my boss could've been in here for this call. "Okay. I'll put the order in right . . . now." I trailed off as my cell phone vibrated with Parker's school on the ID. Fear gripped at my chest and I hurried to get off the phone. "Have a good rest of your week, Mr. Walton."

"Bye now."

"Hello?" I answered my cell as I hung up the office phone, and held my breath.

"Miss Hudson?"

"Yes." *Please, God, please let Parker just be in trouble.*

"This is Assistant Principal Reese from Parker's elementary school."

"Hi, is everything okay?"

"Ma'am, we had to call an ambulance to take Parker to the hos—"

"What?!" I yelled into the phone and stood so fast my desk chair rolled back until it hit the wall.

"They just loaded him up and left a few minutes ago."

I gripped at my head and spun in a tight circle as I tried to think of what I had to do. "Aren't you—aren't you supposed to call me before you just take him to the hospital?"

"He fell off the gym set during the lunch recess and was knocked unconscious, he still hadn't woken up by the time the ambulance left."

I stopped spinning abruptly and my entire body

trembled as I reached blindly for my chair. "W-what? He . . . are you sure it was Parker?"

"Yes, and I'm so sorry to have to be the one to call you. But are you able to go to the hospital, or have another family member meet them there?"

"Is he okay? He's going to be okay right?" I don't know how I'd ended up on the floor, but I couldn't figure out how to get back up. I wasn't seeing anything other than Parker.

The man was silent for a few seconds. "It was a pretty bad fall, Miss Hudson. You should probably get to the hospital. Maybe have someone drive you."

Why wasn't he telling me if Parker would be okay or not? Why was he talking like he wouldn't be? Fat tears quickly fell down my cheeks, and my head jerked to the right when my boss touched my shoulder.

"I'm going," I said into the phone before ending the call and letting my boss help me stand.

"What happened? I heard you—"

"P-parker was rushed—" I cut off on a sob, and pressed down onto Coen's name on my phone. "I have to go."

He just nodded and stepped back as I frantically searched for my purse.

I took off running down the hall and out of the building as Coen's voice mail picked up. Ending the call only to call him again, I begged for him to answer.

Just before I ended the call again, he answered. "Hey, Ray, I'm in the middle of a shoot." He must have heard my sobs because he quickly asked, "Babe, what's wrong?" Panic filled his tone.

"Parker's school called! They said—they said he fell off something on the playground and was unconscious." Another sob burst from my chest as I cranked the engine on my car and pulled out of the parking spot. "He was taken to the hospital by ambulance, he still wasn't waking up by the time they left. He said it was bad, Coen, he couldn't even tell me he was going to be okay!"

Coen's ragged breaths filled the phone. "What? No . . . no."

I choked on my tears, and the sound must have finally broken through Coen's denial.

"Oh my God. I'm on my way."

"Coen, tell me he's going to be okay," I pleaded.

"He's going to be fine, Reagan. He's going to be fine. Babe, you shouldn't be driving. Pull over, let me pick you up."

"No!" I yelled. "I can't sit here and do nothing, I need to get to him. I have to go!"

"Damn it!" he gritted, but I knew by his tone that he'd acknowledged I wouldn't be waiting for him. "Reagan Hudson, listen to me. Keep yourself safe. I'm on my way and I'll meet you there."

I nodded and whispered some sort of good-bye before ending the call and calling my mom. The entire time I prayed Parker would be okay.

Coen—*October 27, 2010*

I PARKED IN the first spot I found, and didn't even bother to check if it was a handicap space or not. I didn't fucking care. They could tow my car if they wanted. I'd already run out on a client after barely telling him why I was leaving, and gone over double the speed limit the entire way . . . a goddamn handicap space wasn't going to stop me from getting in that hospital.

Running into the ER, I looked around the waiting room and rushed to the window when I didn't see Reagan or anyone from her family. "Parker Hudson."

The lady looked at me like I'd just ruined her day before sighing. "Can I help you, sir?"

"Parker Hudson, he was brought in here by ambulance not long ago. Where is he?" Adrenaline was coursing through my body, and I was five seconds from breaking through the locked doors and finding him myself. I didn't know if Reagan had made it here okay, I didn't know if Parker was awake yet . . . I was flipping the fuck out.

Recognition hit her eyes. "His mother just came through here. You can wait out here for now, it's only family allowed back there."

I slammed my hand on the counter. "And he's *my* son, where the fuck is he?!"

The security guard I'd passed when I entered the ER walked up behind me. "Sir, I suggest you calm down."

Looking over my shoulder, I narrowed my eyes at

If he didn't currently look like shit, I would have laughed. "That's right. Because you eat your food."

"Were my parents or brother here yet?" Reagan asked softly.

"No, do you want me to go check?"

She gripped the hand she was still holding harder. "Don't leave," she begged. Sitting carefully on the side of the bed, she cupped Parker's cheek. "How do you feel, honey?"

"Not good."

A pained smile tugged at her lips. "I'm sorry. I wish I could make it go away."

Parker nodded once just as the door opened, and the X-ray technicians walked in. After explaining what they would be doing, and getting ready to take Parker away, he started screaming.

"No! Please, Mommy, don't go!"

"I'm not going anywhere, honey, stop screaming. You're going to make it hurt worse."

"Don't make me go!"

Reagan looked at me helplessly before looking at the techs.

"One of you can come with him, but you'll have to stand outside the room," one of the techs said. "Parker, will you be okay if your mom comes and stands outside the room?"

He groaned, but nodded.

I squeezed her hand before releasing her. "I'll go check to see if your brother's here yet."

"Thank you," she mouthed, and followed them out of the room.

Walking back through the confusing halls, I made it out to the waiting room, and didn't even have time to look for them before all three said my name. Glancing to my left, I walked toward where they were standing from their chairs, and hugged Mrs. Hudson.

"Is he okay?" Keegan asked.

"He's doing fine. A little sick, scared, probably in pain. He doesn't need stitches. They took him back for some X-rays to make sure he didn't crack his skull and to see if there's swelling. Reagan went with him."

The three let out a collective, relieved breath. "So, he's awake?" Mr. Hudson asked.

"Yeah, he'd already woken up by the time I got here."

"Speaking of . . ." Keegan trailed off and raised an eyebrow at me.

I shot him a confused look. "What?"

He cleared his throat and jerked his chin toward the check-in desk behind me. "When Mom and I got here and asked about Parker, the receptionist didn't seem thrilled that more of his family was here. Told us to be assured Parker's parents were with him, and one of them would let us know how Parker was doing. Then she started grumbling about Parker's *dad* almost getting himself thrown out of the hospital for the way he acted."

"She wouldn't tell me where he—" I paused, and jerked my head back. "*Dad*?"

"I love you too," she whispered, and sent me a longing glance before walking out of the room.

Grabbing the chair and moving it closer to the bed, I sat down and looked up at the beeping monitors.

"Hey, Coen?"

"Yeah, bud?" I asked, glancing down to Parker.

"Don't tell Mom, 'kay?"

I bent forward to rest my elbows on the side of his bed. "Don't tell her what?"

"When I woke up here, I was scared because I couldn't find you."

My chest tightened and a lump formed in my throat. "I'm so sorry I wasn't here, bud."

"Mom wasn't here either, but I looked for you." His words were starting to slur, and I didn't know if this was just talk because of the concussion, or if he'd actually been scared because I hadn't been here.

Grabbing the hand closest to me, I squeezed it gently, and looked at his drooping eyes. "I'm here now."

He nodded slowly and blinked heavily before widening his eyes at me. "Love you, Coen."

Thank God I was in a hospital, because I'm pretty sure my heart had just failed. Everything in me seized up, and my heart stuttered after missing a few beats before taking off quickly. The lump in my throat grew, and I couldn't get it to go away. He loved me. I'd called him my son without realizing it. *My* Parker.

"I love you too, Parker," I choked out.

All of the adrenaline from the fear of him not

waking up, trying to be strong for Reagan—even if only for a little while—and all the emotions that had been coursing through my body in just the last ten minutes were suddenly too much. Dropping my head onto the mattress, I let myself cry for the first time in two and a half years.

Reagan—*October 27, 2010*

I STOOD IN the doorway of Parker's room late that night, and watched as Coen lowered him onto his bed before tucking him under the covers. In the three and a half weeks since we'd started letting Parker know that Coen was staying the night, Coen hadn't once put him in bed, or woken him up—and I'm pretty sure it just became my favorite sight in the entire world.

Coen bent down low, placing his hand on the top of Parker's head, and whispered something against it, too low for me to hear.

Never mind. *That* was my favorite sight.

Straightening up, he gave Parker one last look before walking over to where I was waiting on him. I tried to contain the ridiculous smile I knew must have been plastered on my face, but there was no way to. I was so in love with him. I loved the way he loved me, and I *loved* the way he loved my son.

Letting my fingers trail down his forearm, I pushed away from the doorway and walked over to the bed. Pressing my lips to Parker's temple, I brushed back

"That's what we said, she look really nervous. Said you claimed Parker was your son, and then she began describing you at the same time she called security over, probably to have him hunt you down. But when she described you . . . we told her she was correct."

I stood there, not seeing anything as I thought back to my conversation with the woman behind the window. Looking over my shoulder at her, air wheezed out of my lungs. *"And he's* my *son . . ."* Facing Reagan's family again, my face fell. "Oh my God," I muttered, and shakily walked over to one of the chairs.

"Are you okay?" Mrs. Hudson asked as she took the chair next to me.

I stared down at the tile below me and just focused on pulling air into my body.

"Steele." I looked up to find Keegan smirking. "You doin' okay there?"

"I hadn't even realized . . ." I trailed off and shook my head.

His smirk morphed into a full-blown smile. "I can see that."

I barely glanced at Mrs. Hudson to see her smiling at me with her eyes watering, before looking back at the floor. I stayed like that for minutes as I tried to figure out what had happened, and how I couldn't have even realized what I'd been saying. I wanted to say it was because I was scared, or because I knew Reagan needed me, and the lady hadn't been about to let me back there . . . but that wasn't it. It hadn't been a calculated response; it'd just been the first thing that left my lips when she tried to keep me from Parker. My Parker.

"I need to get back there," I said suddenly, and stood. Looking at the three of them, I tried not to notice how differently they were all watching me now. Like they knew what I'd just come to realize, and were happy.

I was happy. I was also scared as shit.

"I'll let you know what the doctor says." Turning, I walked back to the doors and waited for them to let me through.

Reagan's soft voice drifted out of the room, so I stopped before I got to the doorway. Taking deep breaths in, I ran my hands over my face, and hoped like hell that she wouldn't notice a difference in me.

"Hey." She smiled. "I'm guessing they're out there?"

"Yeah, sorry it took me so long to get back."

She waved off the apology and looked at Parker. "Please don't be sorry. Do you mind sitting in here with him while I go talk to my parents really quick?"

As long as they didn't tell her what I'd said. "Go for it."

"Okay, they light is still bothering him, but he needs to stay awake." Reagan leaned up on her toes to kiss me. "Thank you for getting here so fast, Coen. I—as soon as I got the call, I just knew I needed you. So, thank you."

"Don't thank me, Reagan." I cradled her face in my hands and kissed her once more. "I love you. I'm always here when you need me."

Chapter Eleven

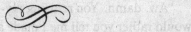

Coen—*November 1, 2010*

I WAS FROWNING by the time Saco's wife, Olivia, was done ranting and bitching loud enough that I'd begun to wonder if she was trying to let me hear her.

Saco groaned. "Sorry, man."

Waiting until I made sure I wouldn't tell him he'd made a mistake in marrying her, I asked, "What was that about this time?"

"She took what little savings I had after buying the house, and put it down on a brand-new Mercedes yesterday without telling me. When she came back, she got pissed that I wasn't happy *for her* and took off to her parents' house."

"Are you serious?"

"I don't know how I'm supposed to be happy about her draining our savings, and then giving us a car payment I can't afford." He let out a long sigh. "Anyway, that was her, just coming back from her parents'. I'd had to go out and buy formula last night so I could feed Tate."

I wouldn't say it. I would. Not. Say. It. "I'm sorry, Brody."

"Aw, damn. You're using my first name, I think I would rather you tell me I made a mistake."

"Are you a mind reader now?"

He laughed, but it still sounded off. "Nah, I just know you. Tell me something to get my mind off her bullshit. How are you and Reagan?"

I didn't want to sit there and brag about my relationship when the only good thing to come from Saco's was his son, but I knew he needed the distraction. "We're great, to be honest. Things have . . . I don't know. So much has changed."

"Good or bad?"

"Good. Every day that passes I know more and more that I need them, and I don't know what I would do without them. I hate that they don't live with me, I can't stand the fact that they aren't my family. I don't know how it happened, but I love that kid, and I love his mom so damn much. I want to marry her. I want to adopt—"

"Whoa, wait." Saco cut me off. "What? I knew you were really into her, but didn't the two of you just start dating a few months ago?"

I paused and thought for a second. "No."

"Yeah, Steele, it's only been a few months. I've

some of his blond hair and tried to remember him just like this. There'd been no crack on his skull, and no major swelling; the doctor had told us he'd been incredibly lucky. And I was so thankful for whoever was looking over my son.

"I'm so glad you're okay," I whispered. "I love you, baby."

With one last kiss to his forehead, I stood and walked into Coen's waiting arms. I inhaled sharply when he grabbed the backs of my thighs and pulled me up, but quickly wrapped my hands around his neck, and legs around his hips.

His dark eyes stayed locked on mine as he walked us out of Parker's bedroom and into mine—leaving both doors open. Letting me slide down his body, his fingers went to my pants, but there was no heat in his dark eyes tonight. I stepped out of them when they pooled at my feet, and raised my arms when he began pulling my shirt over my head. Leaving my camisole on, he reached inside to unhook my bra, and worked it off before dropping it on the floor as well. Taking a step away from me, he took off his jeans and shirt, leaving himself in only his boxer briefs, and reached for my hand. He brushed his lips slowly across mine while his eyes still held mine captive—and in them I saw everything I was feeling being reflected back on me. The fear, the craving, the love, the trust.

Walking to the bed, he turned off the lamp, flipped back the covers, and slid in before pulling me in with him. Curling his body around mine, he pressed his

lips to my shoulder as the arm under me moved so
his hand was flat against my stomach, and the other
moved until it was over my heart.

No words, and yet he'd said so much. So much that
I agreed with wholeheartedly.

I was his.

I wasn't going anywhere.

And I was so in love with him too.

you and your mom?" He nodded. "That's the kind of shooting I'm doing."

"Oh, yeah. That was cool."

I smiled at him. "It was cool."

"Well we'll go so you can get back to it," Reagan said as she put a hand on Parker's shoulder to pull him back. "Are you coming over tonight?"

"I planned on it," I said each word slowly as I judged her reaction.

"Okay, I'm exhausted from today—"

Disappointment quickly flooded my chest, but I refused to let her see it. "Then I'll see you tomorrow."

She laughed and placed a hand on my chest. "I meant, I'm exhausted in that I'm just going to be ordering takeout instead of cooking. Please come over."

"Takeout sounds perfect, and maybe bed early and I'll take care of you since you're so exhausted . . ." I raised an eyebrow and she blushed.

"Coen," she chastised.

"Drive safe, Duchess, I'll see you soon."

After a quick light-saber stabbing from Parker and a kiss from Reagan, they left my studio, and I just stood there staring at the door they'd walked through.

"I didn't know you were married."

I turned to look at my client and laughed awkwardly. "Uh, I'm not. That's my girlfriend."

He looked over at the door, and a look crossed his face like that had explained it all. "Got it! Now I don't feel bad thinking that kid had probably been the result of the milkman."

My face dropped and hands clenched into fists, but I forced myself to laugh again. "You ready to finish this?"

"Yeah, but, Coen . . . I wouldn't be looking out for you if I didn't say this." He put his hands on his hips and looked at me like he was about to deliver the worst news possible.

I steadied myself and crossed my arms over my chest as I waited for him to continue. I still hadn't completely ruled out punching him.

"I dated this girl for a while who had a daughter. I was cool with her kid, the girl was a total sweetheart. Next thing I know my girlfriend's pregnant and freaking out, saying she can't have another kid by herself. She tried so damn hard to get me to marry her before she had the baby; but that wasn't about to happen. And thank God it didn't. Found out after the kid was born that he wasn't even mine. My girlfriend had to do a paternity test to find out *who* the father was because she had been fucking four different guys. Trying to get one of us to marry her because she wanted someone to help her raise her first kid. And she'd sworn up and down she was on the pill. I believed her, trusted her, loved her and her daughter . . ."

My forehead bunched together. "What exactly are you getting at?"

He held up his hands like he was surrendering. "I'm not trying to piss you off, and your girlfriend

"Want to guess who that is?"

His smile got wider before he took off running for the door. "Coen! Did you have fun shooting that guy?"

I laughed and sighed. We somehow needed to get Parker off that whole "shooting" thing.

"Uh . . . yeah. I did."

"Are you gonna stay tonight? I want you to take me to school tomorrow."

I raised an eyebrow as they rounded the corner into the living room. Parker's excitement was quickly draining from his face, and Coen looked like someone had just punched him in the stomach.

"Yeah, I don't know about that. We'll talk about it later."

Parker shot me a confused look, and I tried to compose my expression, but didn't catch it in time. He looked back and forth between us before walking over to stand next to me.

I took a step toward Coen, but stopped when his near-black eyes met mine. "Are you feeling okay? Did something happen?"

"No, I'm fine," he clipped out, his voice rough and low.

I glanced down at Parker when he wrapped an arm around my hip, and looked back at Coen—who was now looking in the kitchen. Clearing my throat, I tried to ease the awkward tension that had settled. "Well, do you have something in particular you want for dinner?"

"Whatever you want," he mumbled.

"Coen."

He looked back at me and shrugged. "I said whatever you want, Ray. Order what you want."

My eyes widened and my lips parted. He wasn't raising his voice, but this Coen . . . well I'd never seen this Coen.

"Are you mad at Mom?" Parker asked from by my side, and my chest started aching right then.

Parker hadn't asked Coen if he was being mean to me since the very first time he met him, and he'd never asked if Coen was mad at me. If he was catching onto the weighted feel to the room too, then I knew it wasn't my imagination, and I hated that he was witnessing this at all—whatever *this* was.

"Parker, honey, can you go to your room so I can talk to Coen?"

Coen shot me a look like he didn't understand why I would want to talk, and Parker moved in front of me and tilted his head back to better see me.

"But he's mad at you," he said softly.

I put a smile on my face for him and ran my hand through his hair. "No, he's not, but I do need to talk to him. Just adults, so can you go to your room until I come get you? You can take my iPad and play your games on there," I added when he didn't look like he would budge.

"Okay!" Running over to grab my iPad from off the couch, he took off for his room and shut the door.

"Co—"

Locking my jaw when it began quivering, I curled my hands into fists. I would. Not. Cry.

He was no better than Austin. If he didn't want us, then it was his loss. We didn't need him, we were fine alone.

Alone after experiencing life with Coen seemed impossible, and that one word had me falling to the floor as a strained sob burst from my chest.

Reaching into my back pocket, I pulled out my phone and tapped on the screen a few times before putting it to my ear. My body shook relentlessly as I tried to hold back the sobs, and they just pushed through harder.

"Hey, Ray."

"Kee-Keegan," I choked out.

"What's wrong?" he shouted.

"I need y-you . . . here. I need you here."

I heard shuffling and keys. "Are you at your apartment? I'm coming, what happened?"

Strained cries were all that left me for long moments. "Yes, just please."

"I'm coming."

Putting the phone on the ground, I wrapped my arms around my waist, as if it could somehow hold me together. It didn't. It felt like I was breaking, and I didn't know how to even begin to pick up all those pieces of me—of us.

"Mom?"

I looked quickly to the right into Parker's wide eyes, and tried so hard to stop the tears. But seeing him only made it worse. My heartache for my son was only just beginning, and it was worse than anything I had begun to feel for myself.

"Did Coen go back to his house?"

When I couldn't speak, I just nodded, and Parker seemed to accept that and sat on the floor next to me.

"He'll come back," he said softly.

If I could have stopped the crying to take care of my son right then, I still wouldn't have been able to respond to that. Because even if Coen tried to come back, I wasn't sure I would let him.

Coen—*November 1, 2010*

MY PHONE RANG for the fifth time in a row, and as I reached down to shut it off, I caught sight of Saco's name, and answered.

"Hel—"

"You just left them? What the fuck is wrong with you?" he yelled, cutting me off.

"Christ, did Hudson call you?"

"Yeah, he did. And, Steele, he's fucking pissed and coming after you."

I groaned and tightened my grip on the steering wheel. I'd been driving around for hours. Not knowing or caring where I was going . . . just going in circles. "I wouldn't expect anything else from him."

"I don't understand, we just talked like, six hours

with the girl, you'd use that shit against me? Question me as a man and soldier? Fuck. You. Saco."

"No, and you know I'm not. From what you and Hudson have said, and what I've seen . . . I know this isn't just a relationship for you. This is your future, and you're being a bitch because you had a moment where you let your fears and insecurities get to you. Do you think I don't have days where I'm terrified that I'm gonna fuck up? That Tate could have a better dad than me? Just because I worry, doesn't mean I'm going to leave my son."

"Parker isn't my son."

"Wow. Coming from the guy who not even a week ago claimed Parker as his son without a second thought. Hudson told me about that too, asshole." There was a beat of silence before Saco sighed. "He's not your blood, but that's your son. From the way you said that, I know you don't even believe the shit you're saying."

I didn't, and I wanted to die for even letting the thought cross my mind.

I'd spent that night, and the next day, in my studio trying to edit. Trying to do anything to get my mind off Reagan and Parker. Nothing was helping. I'd been the one to get scared and leave them. I'd been the one to call it off before any of us could get more invested. But now I felt hollow.

I couldn't go back to my place without seeing them there, and here, in the studio, flashes of Reagan and I together were hitting me hard.

I hadn't slept for more than thirty minutes last night before I'd woken in a panic, completely drenched in sweat. And this time, it hadn't been flashbacks of my time in the army. There hadn't been a flashback, nightmare, or dream . . . just the sense that I'd physically lost both Parker and Reagan and couldn't find them.

Hudson was calling me every few hours to yell at me, and though I'd grabbed my phone to call Reagan over a dozen times, I hadn't gone through with it and she'd never tried to get ahold of me.

My phone rang, and I grabbed for it quickly. Disappointment and regret poured through me when I saw Saco's name instead of Reagan's. My thumb hovered over the red button before I gave in and hit the green.

"Hello?" Nothing came from the other side. "Saco, you there?"

A pained cry sounded, and I looked at the screen on my phone to confirm it *was* Saco, before I tried talking to him again.

"You there? What's wrong?"

Silence greeted me for long seconds, and just as I started to say something again, his strangled voice came over the line. "He's gone."

"What? Who's gone?" Panic filled me thinking about Parker. But I tried to calm myself, knowing Hudson or Reagan would have been the one to call me about that.

"He's gone—it's all my fault—he's gone."

"What happened, Saco, who's gone?"

"Don't let them go," Saco said minutes later, his voice hoarse.

"What?"

"My son is gone, St—" he broke off with a cry. "I can't get him back. You can . . . don't let them go."

"Brody, what can I do? I'll get on the first flight to Oregon, I swear. But what can I do?"

"Just don't let yours go. Promise me."

"I'm not. I can't let them go." I grabbed a shirt and threw it on over my head before searching for my wallet and keys. "I'm so sorry. I'll get Hudson, and we'll be out there as soon as we can, all right? I'll call you when I know details."

"He can't be gone," he whispered.

Knowing there was nothing I could say, and that he needed someone now, I kept him on the phone as I left for Hudson's apartment, and continued to listen to him cry until he told me his brother had just shown up and ended the call. Hudson hated me right now, but I knew I'd fucked up and was prepared to do anything to make it right again. But right now I was fighting with myself over whom to go to first. Reagan, or Saco. I needed to see her just as much as I needed to get to Oregon.

Like Saco last night, all that was going through my head was the definition of the warrior ethos from The Soldier's Creed. "I will never quit," is followed immediately by, "I will never leave a fallen comrade." Those words went much deeper than the obvious, and right now, Saco was struggling. We needed to be there for him.

Pulling up outside Hudson's building, I kept my car running and ran up the stairs to his apartment. I started banging on the door immediately, and didn't stop until it opened.

I tried to dodge the flying fist too late and stumbled back as my hand went to my jaw.

"What do you want, you piece of shit?" he growled, and the look on his face was clear. He wanted to murder me.

"I know you're pissed, I know. I'll talk to you about that, but right now we need to buy tickets and get to Oregon."

He hadn't been expecting that, and his anger faded to confusion as his head jerked back. "Oregon? What—why?"

"Saco didn't call you?"

Hudson stepped back and let me in, and I ran over to the kitchen table where his laptop was open and sat down. God*damn*, my jaw fucking hurt.

"I talked to him yesterday . . . what the fuck are you doing? I don't want you in here, and I sure as shit don't want you on my damn laptop. You *ruined* my little sister."

I slammed my hand down on the table and stood back up. "I *know* that, Hudson. I. Fucking. Know. I made the biggest mistake of my life yesterday, but right now Saco needs us. He got in a wreck this morning with his son. Dude, Tate died. Saco's so fucked up right now."

I can. Because of them . . . you're toxic. I can't have someone like you in my son's life."

I stumbled back a step like she'd hit me, and watched her get in her car and drive away as my legs threatened to give out beneath me.

My entire world was being ripped away from me, and once again, I was the only one to blame.

Chapter Thirteen

Coen—*December 5, 2010*

A PAINED GROWL left me as I flew into a sitting position and gripped the sheets below me. Looking around me, I bent forward and dropped my head into my hands as I tried to push the memories from my mind.

"God damn it!" I roared, and launched a pillow across the room.

Jerkily untangling myself from the sheets, I pulled my clothes off and turned the water on as hot as it could go. Waiting until steam billowed out, I stepped into the shower and fisted my hands against the burning sting. I needed it. I needed it to make the smell, pain, noise, and clear-as-day memories go away.

Stepping out, I didn't even bother grabbing a towel to dry myself as I searched for clothes and my running shoes. By the time I had everything on, was out my door, and already running on the path, I still had water dripping down my body. I didn't care that I was only in shorts and a short-sleeved shirt, and that it was snowing, I just needed to run. I needed to forget.

That was almost laughable.

I would never forget.

A deep, searing pain pierced my chest as I came closer to the playground in the park, and my footsteps automatically slowed down. Even in the dark gray of the early day, I could see the times Reagan and I had brought Parker here. See the first time I'd accidentally run into her here. And each one made the ache in my body grow as it had every time I made it out this far.

Three and a half weeks since I'd seen Reagan. Almost five since I'd seen Parker, and I hadn't even told him I loved him that day. I'd been an asshole, and left. That was it, the last memory he had of me.

Lying down on my back in the snow, I stared up at the lightening sky and tried to remember every moment with them.

I hadn't stopped calling Reagan, and she hadn't started answering. But I hadn't shown up at her work or apartment anymore—to be honest, I was afraid of what I would find out if I did.

That she had moved on. That she had hardened herself to men again. That she had meant her words about me being toxic, about not wanting someone like me in her son's life. That she still believed I only wanted her so I wouldn't have to deal with my demons . . . I would wake up the same way I had this morning every day for the rest of my life if it meant getting Reagan and Parker back.

I wish I could say that because of Reagan shutting me out, I'd gone to get help—well, *tried* to get help. But I hadn't. I still believed talking to some random psychiatrist wouldn't do shit, but every day I wished I would have opened up to Reagan when I'd had the chance. She understood me. She knew just by looking at pictures I'd taken of myself what I was doing, when I hadn't even realized that I'd been doing it. She didn't judge me. Hadn't . . . *hadn't* judged me. She would have listened; and my peace—in the form of the most amazing girl I'd ever met—would have helped me somehow.

I lay there thinking about words that should have been said long ago . . . back when she'd first looked through all my pictures. But it was too late; I couldn't turn back time to change what I had kept from her.

Pictures. I sat up from the cold, wet ground and stared blankly in front of me. Not seeing the playground in front of me. Scrambling to my feet, I took off in a dead sprint for my condo, never once slowing down until I was back inside.

Grabbing my laptop, I quickly found the folder with the pictures of me and scrolled through them before opening up another folder, and then another.

I sat there staring at the pictures in front of me for long moments before running around my condo to find my phone, and calling Hudson.

There was a grumbling noise, and it was only then

that I realized I didn't even know what time it was. But I didn't fucking care.

"Hudson, I need your help," I said breathlessly.

There was a rustling noise for a few seconds before: "Steele? What happened?"

"I gotta get my family back, and I need your help."

Reagan—*December 16, 2010*

"KEEGAN," I WHINED, and fumbled with the blindfold. "This is so dumb, why can't you just tell me where we're going?"

Someone smacked my arm. "Stop trying to take it off, can't you try to have fun just once?" Erica asked.

Crossing my arms, I huffed as I sat back against the seat. "I have fun . . . I would just rather not be kidnapped by my brother and his girlfriend."

"But it's for your birthday, so it's allowed, and a surprise, and *fun*," she argued. "So get over it."

"Seriously, Ray, just a few more minutes until we're there."

I made a face at the direction of my brother's voice. "I would have tried to guess where we were going if you hadn't confused me by going up and down the fucking freeway."

"Are you really being a bitch on your birthday?" Keegan asked. "Because this is not a party and you cannot cry."

"Who said I'm crying? I'm not crying. I just want

to know where I'm being hauled off to before you kill me. I would've liked to say good-bye to my son. Speaking of! Why isn't he in the car with us?"

"Did you really want him to be bored while I drove up and down the freeway for an hour? Besides, you heard him, he asked to stay with Mom and Dad."

With a defeated sigh, I mumbled, "No."

But honestly? Even though I loved my family for whatever they had planned for my twenty-third birthday, I just wanted to be in my apartment with Parker. It was nothing against my family . . . I just didn't want to do much of anything lately. Each day seemed harder than the last to function. To get myself out of bed. To go to work. The only thing that drove me to do anything was Parker. Even with tonight, I'd known we would be going out to celebrate, but Erica had taken one look at me and shoved me back in my apartment before doing my hair and makeup, and making me change. Saying I had to at least look like I was excited to be celebrating. Its not like I'd been in sweats . . . actually, yeah, I had.

All I wanted was to make it through another night so I could crawl into bed and finally give in to the ache of not having Coen there, not having his arms wrapped around me, and knowing he wouldn't be there in the morning to wake up Parker with me.

I tried telling myself I'd made the right decision in not letting him back into our lives, but when Austin had left me, I'd gotten stronger every day without him. I felt like I was slowly dying without Coen. After

"This wasn't your fault," I told him a few minutes
later. "There's nothing you could have—"

"Don't let them go," Saco mumbled. "They could
be gone tomorrow. Be with them, enjoy them, love
them while they're here."

I nodded but didn't respond. I didn't want to talk
about Reagan and Parker with him now, not when we
were staring at his son's grave. I didn't want to talk
about what I'd thrown away, and was trying so hard
to get back, when the person he loved most in the
world was gone.

Instead, I took a step back, knowing he wasn't
ready to leave this place yet. Glancing at Hudson,
he gave me a look and I nodded. We'd have to take
Saco from here soon, or he'd drive himself crazy. He
needed to keep grieving, but he needed to do it away
from where he looked like he was about to lie down
and never leave.

I'd called Reagan at least a dozen times a day every
day since I'd shown up at Hudson's place, but she'd
never once picked up. Hudson had even let me use
his phone, but she'd hung up the second she heard
my voice. And every time, I felt like I was closer and
closer to losing them for good.

After I told Hudson about the call from Saco and
the story about my client's relationship, and how those
conversations had started the worries and insecurities
that had snowballed out of control into what went
down in Reagan's apartment, he'd understood. He'd
punched me again the second we got out of the airport

in Oregon, but he'd understood. He knew I'd made a mistake, and he knew I'd do anything to get them back. But there was only so much I could do while I was a couple states away, and right now, Hudson and I needed to be there for our brother.

Reagan—*November 7, 2010*

MY BODY STIFFENED when I felt my phone start vibrating in my back pocket. Looking over to where Parker was playing with my dad, I pulled the phone out and locked my jaw when Coen's name, and a picture of the two of us flashed on the screen.

I sat there staring at the screen until the voice mail finally picked up, and a deep sense of longing filled me—as it did every time he called.

"Are you ever going to answer that boy's calls?"

My head jerked up to where my mom was staring at me from across the table, and my brow furrowed. "*Ever*? Don't say that like it's been years or something. It hasn't even been a week."

"That doesn't answer my question, sweetheart. He's called you five times since you got here this morning, and I know that's not unusual for him right now."

She was counting? Pressing down the lock button, I held it until I could turn my phone off. Parker was here, I was with my parents, and Keegan was with . . .

Looking at my son smiling as he played on the floor—completely oblivious to everything happening around him—I shook my head sadly as a few tears slipped down my cheeks. "You must've been mistaken."

Coen—*November 10, 2010*

IT'D BEEN ALMOST a week and a half since I'd walked out of Reagan's apartment, and even though I still called at least twelve times a day, she wasn't talking to me.

Hudson and I had come home from Oregon late Sunday night because Hudson had to be at work again on Monday, and even with trying to catch Reagan at her apartment, I hadn't seen her either. Now I was outside the building she worked in, parked next to her car, and was waiting for her to walk outside at any moment.

The second she walked outside I stepped out of my car and waited for her to see me. Her hazel eyes briefly glossed over me before doing a double take, and she froze on the middle of the sidewalk. With a step back, she froze again, and I watched as her chest started rising and falling roughly.

I knew she needed to get to her car. She needed to go get Parker from school, so she couldn't just avoid me, and it was clear in her eyes. She wanted to run, but she knew she couldn't.

Walking to where she still hadn't moved from, I stopped in front of her and looked into her lifeless eyes. "Please talk to me. You've been avoiding me for over a week, and there's so much I need to say."

She didn't respond. Her face had no emotion, just like her eyes. And it was killing me to know I'd made her look like that.

"I was wrong to say what I said, I was wrong to try to make you think you were the problem. I was freaking out and—" I cut off when she quickly tried to walk around me, and I caught hold of her arm. "Reagan, please! I'm sorry, I know I fucked up. I know that. I got scared for a split second, that doesn't mean you should just shut me out."

She turned on me, and I hated that instead of sadness or anger, I saw pity in her eyes. "*Me* shut *you* out? You ran from us, Coen, what do you expect from me?"

I nodded and let go of her to run my hands roughly over my head. "For a *second*. I ran for a goddamn *second*. I love you, Reagan. I love Parker. Don't take the two of you from me."

Biting down on her bottom lip, she shook her head slowly as she began turning back around. "You did that all by yourself."

"Reagan, I am right here, and I am begging you not to do this. Just talk to me about what happened, let me explain, and for Christ's sake, stop acting like you don't care."

well, he was with friends. No one would need to get in touch with me who couldn't wait.

"Reagan," Mom prompted.

"No, Mom, I don't think I will ever answer his calls."

The disappointment was clear on her face and in her tone. "He said he needed time to think. He said he needed some space. To me, that's not even asking for a break, maybe he just wanted to be alone for a little while, and you took it the wrong way."

I raised my eyebrows and brought my hand up to point at myself, but didn't make it all the way before pointing at my phone instead. My jaw shook as I whispered, "I took it the wrong way?" Clearing my throat, I straightened in the chair and shook my head. "No, I didn't take anything the wrong way. Those were *some* of the words he said, but his meaning was crystal clear."

"Reagan, you push men away, it's what you do."

"I pushed him, and he pushed right back. I stopped pushing him months ago. I did not want him to leave, Mom. You have no idea how much it destroyed me to watch him walk away from us."

She leaned forward and extended her arm on the table toward me. "But he's calling. He's calling all the time. That doesn't sound like a man who doesn't want you."

Neither did his voice mails. "He walked away once, Mom. That's all I need to know."

"Reagan. You tried walking away in the beginning too."

An agitated huff blew past my lips and I rolled my eyes. "To protect my son. Not because I didn't want a relationship."

"That's not fair."

"Whose side are you on, Mom?"

"Parker's," she said without missing a beat. "I'm on Parker's. I want the world for you, Reagan, but you're being childish. I had my reservations about Coen in the beginning, but he is the best thing to ever happen to you and my grandson. And, yes, he made a mistake, but he's trying to come back, and you're stopping him. You're stopping my grandson from having the father he deserves."

"If Austin had tried coming back, would you have wanted me to give him another chance?"

My mom scoffed. "Of course not. But he didn't love you the way you deserve to be loved, and he did not love Parker. Coen claimed Parker as his son without a second thought, and without realizing it, the day Parker was rushed to the ER. Even when we mentioned it to him, he still didn't catch it for a few seconds. That is why I *know* he deserves another chance."

I sat there in shock for a few moments before I was able to compose myself. And just when I started to ask my mom what exactly had happened, Coen's words drifted through my mind. *"I'm not your husband, he's not my fucking child. It is not my job to take care of you!"*

a month of constant calling, his calls had stopped a week and a half ago; and while a part of me was glad for it, the rest was terrified that I would never hear from him again. And I didn't know what was making it worse. That it was *my* decision. That I knew it was *still* killing Parker to not have Coen there. Or that I'd purposefully hurt Coen to the point where I'd hoped he would *want* to stay away.

So, no, I didn't want to be kidnapped. I didn't want to be separated from my son. I wanted to be home with him acting like there wasn't a huge piece of us missing.

The car stopped and I straightened when I heard the gears shift to park. "Are we here?" I grabbed for the blindfold, and my arms were smacked away again.

"You have to keep it on until we're inside," Erica chastised.

"Is that necessary?"

"Yes!" they both hissed, and I jerked back.

"Got it. Sorry."

I let Erica help me out of the car and waited until she grabbed my hand to lead me into the restaurant.

"Parker's already here?"

"Your guy is waiting for you," she said patiently. "There's a *tiny* step up right in front of you."

I stepped up and my brow furrowed when the light behind the blindfold vanished. I knew we were inside. But it was completely silent, and it sure as hell didn't smell like food.

"Uh . . ."

"I'll be right back, let me help Keegan with your gift. Don't move!"

"Erica!" I complained, and reached out into the darkness, letting my arms drop when I heard a door shut. "Seriously?"

Taking a deep breath, my body stilled and goose bumps rose on my arms as the faint scent of the building I was in registered in my mind. I knew this place. I knew that smell.

Quick flashes tortured me. Skin against skin. Perfectly placed arms and lips. Fingers slowly pulling down the zipper on my jeans. A firm hand gripping my hair. A large bed. Slow movements as I fell in love with *him*.

My lips barely parted and the goose bumps moved to my entire body as the flashes kept coming. Taking a step back, my hands moved to the blindfold, but stopped halfway when a song began playing throughout the space. As I ripped the blindfold off, my mouth dropped open and I hurried to cover it with my hand when I saw everything in front of me.

I was in Coen's studio, and hanging from the ceiling were large canvases. Dozens of them. They were low enough so the canvases hung directly in front of me in two rows set across from each other at an angle.

I walked past picture after picture of Coen. Every one I'd seen the day I looked through the folder of him. They still gripped at my heart when I saw his eyes or his face covered, knowing that he was hiding his demons from the world, but that never took away from how amazing each one was.

My footsteps faltered when the pictures changed to the flashes I'd just been having. The photo shoot Coen and I had done right here in this studio was now in front of me. In each picture the chemistry between us was tangible. In each picture the passion and love that kept pulling us together was breaking my heart more and more. Tears filled my eyes before spilling over as I came upon pictures from the park of Coen and Parker, Parker and me, Coen and me together . . . and last, the three of us.

I stopped walking and looked straight ahead at the only canvas on an easel, which was situated at the end, in between the two rows. Coen was leaning in to kiss me, both of his hands cupping my cheeks; one of my hands was resting on his chest while the other held Parker close to me. Parker's head was tilted back, looking up at us with a large smile on his face—and there, across our feet, were the words: *My Peace*.

A jolt went through my body when Coen's voice came from directly behind me, and I bit down on my lip to try to stop the fresh wave of tears.

"Two and a half years ago, I was on a mission and my team was ambushed. I'd fallen through a trap and was knocked unconscious, and when I woke up, the five of us were in a small room."

I didn't turn to face him as he spoke. I just shut my eyes and listened to each soft, haunted word he was sharing with me.

"We were each chained to the ceiling and floor, and roughly an hour after I woke, four men came into the room with us. One by one they tortured my men for hours in ways I refuse to plague your world with, before finally giving them the relief of shooting them. They didn't want information, and they never said anything to us. They tortured them just for the sake of torturing them. Saco's team came in at the exact same moment they killed the last man on my team."

A silent sob worked its way through my body, and my shoulders jerked from the force of it. I shook my head and fought the craving to reach behind me to touch him, to be there for him while he relived this.

"I'd promised their wives I would bring them home safe, and I didn't keep that promise. I watched them die, and it was because *I* fell into a trap I know I should have seen."

"No," I choked out.

"I see that day whenever I fall asleep. I see it whenever a smell or sound triggers it," he continued, his voice still slow and dark. "I didn't think I deserved happiness, not after that, and not until I met you."

The tips of his fingers brushed up the arm that hung at my side, and my breath caught from the intimacy of the simple gesture.

"You changed me so completely. I've tried to hide—and hide from—my demons. It wasn't until you that I stopped hiding. I fell in love with you and your son, Reagan. I fell hard, and fast, and everything about the three of us together made sense. But I let a few words form doubt, and I know I shattered your trust—I know I shattered the little trust you already

"It's not that I don't care, I'm protecting *him*," she ground out as she kept walking.

"I thought we were done with that bullshit. I thought we were done with you pushing me away because you're scared of what could happen in the future."

She didn't stop walking, and she didn't look back at me.

"Reagan, talk to me!"

"You're right," she said, and suddenly whirled on me. "We are done with all that bullshit. We were done with it the day you told me you couldn't promise me a forever."

"Babe—"

"You were right about that too, Coen." Straightening her back, she hardened her hazel eyes at me. "You couldn't promise me a forever any more than I could promise you one. And I'm not taking us away from you because I'm scared you'll run. You already fucking ran, Coen. You already ran, and now you're regretting it because you lost the one thing that could silence your demons."

My body went rigid and my eyes narrowed. "Excuse me?"

She huffed a sad laugh, and that look of pity deepened. "I don't know why it took me so long to figure it out. I was so consumed in everything you are—and so blinded by the bullshit you fed me—that I never really noticed *why* you fought so hard for us. It wasn't because you loved Parker. It wasn't because you loved me. It was because I chased away what you can't escape in here," she said, and touched my temple with her fingers. "It was because I was a means to forget about all that for a little while."

"That's bullshit."

"You told me—"

"I know what I fucking said, Ray! And it's true—you do silence them. But that is not why I fought for us. You completely captivated me because of what being near you can do to me, but I fought for us because I fucking loved you. I've always loved you. I want to marry you, I want to adopt Parker so I can legally be his dad, I want to give you as much of a forever as I have."

She shook her head sadly and stepped away from me. "And there you go trying to blind me with your words again. You're an artist, Coen, through and through. What you see of the world through your camera, and the words that come from your mouth. But I'm not buying it anymore. I'm done letting you use us so you can have a few moments of peace from your fucked-up mind."

My head jerked back and mouth opened, but nothing came out.

"The demons in there?" she said after taking a couple steps away. "They're ruining you. You've allowed them so much freedom that they now control your life. And you may not be able to see it, Coen, but

He cut me off with a hard kiss. "Don't apologize. God, *please* don't."

"I love you, Coen; Parker loves you, we need you."

His dark eyes held mine as he promised, "I swear to you I'm not going anywhere again."

I nodded and spoke through the tightness in my throat. "I know."

He started walking back toward the studio with me still in his arms as he whispered, "I love you. I'm going to marry you, and adopt Parker. I'm going to give you that forever, Reagan."

As we reached the door, Erica spoke up. "Don't worry about tonight. Parker's spending the night with your parents, just have fun."

I sent her a grateful look, and just barely caught my brother's horrified expression as Coen walked us inside.

"Don't have too much fun!"

Coen just shut and locked the door behind us, before capturing my mouth again and walking us slowly through his studio. Letting me slide down his body, he helped me take off his shirt and pants without ever once stopping his advance. By the time we made it to the large bed, my bra was being dropped to the floor and he was pulling off my underwear as he gently pushed me down onto the bed.

As I slid to the middle of the bed, my body heated and stomach tightened. He crawled on top of me and positioned himself between my legs. Grabbing one of my hands, he intertwined our fingers as he slid inside me, and I audibly exhaled at the feel of him again. I'd missed this connection. Missed the way his body felt against mine. Missed the way the muscles in his arms and back tensed and shuddered below my fingertips as he controlled our movements. Missed the way shivers ran up my spine as his lips ghosted over the most sensitive parts of my body. Missed the way his dark eyes conveyed more emotion than any words ever could.

"I love you," he whispered, the words sounding like a promise as my fingers tightened around his and a surge of heat rushed through my body seconds before he followed me into his own release.

We stayed in each other's arms, talking softly as our bodies relaxed over the next few minutes, and I wondered how I ever thought I could live without this man, and was so thankful that he never once gave up on me.

"I want to stay here all night with you," he admitted as he pulled me onto his chest. "But what would you think to getting dressed, picking up Parker, and going out to dinner as a family? We have to celebrate your birthday."

Somehow, more tears filled my eyes as a wide smile slowly crossed my face, and I kissed him roughly before sitting up, pulling him with me. "Thank you for understanding me."

His lips tilted up in a crooked smile and he shook his head before his dark eyes met mine. "If only you knew how backward that thank-you was, Duchess."

"Shit," he whispered, and pressed his fists onto the table, dropping his head. "You're lying, right?"

"I wish I was."

Straightening, he ran his hands over his face, and stood there staring at nothing for a few minutes before responding. "All right. Get us the first flight out of here, do you want my card?"

"No, I got it."

"I'm gonna pack and call Erica, she's at work right now." He'd turned to head to his room, and turned right back around with a finger pointed at me. "This doesn't change shit between us, you get me?"

I didn't respond. I knew this wouldn't change anything, and there was no point in responding to him. No matter what I said right now, we would end up fighting about it . . . and this wasn't the time.

Chapter Twelve

Coen—*November 5, 2010*

HUDSON AND I stood back behind Saco for almost an hour after everyone had left the cemetery. The service had been short, and painfully heartbreaking, but nothing could compare as we watched the world's smallest coffin be lowered into the ground.

There was nothing like it. No words to describe it.

Olivia screaming that Brody was a murderer had only served to have her hauled off by her father, and to have Brody collapse on himself as grief consumed him.

Never in my life had I wanted to hit a woman until that moment.

Stepping forward, I put a hand on Saco's shoulder, and waited to see if he would respond. He didn't. He stood there, still as stone, staring at the fresh mound of dirt.

ago. You told me you wanted to adopt Parker. Fuck, Steele, you told me you wanted to marry her!"

"I know, I—"

"How can something like that change so drastically in just *hours*?"

"I freaked, okay? I was thinking about all of it, and I—it just scared the shit out of me. You were right, I went from not wanting anything steady to wanting to get married and adopt a six-year-old in less than three months. Who does that? I just. Fucking. Freaked."

"But I wasn't trying to get you to leave them! I was trying to get you to not rush into a marriage! You could have called me and talked to me about it before just up and leaving her with no warning."

I kept talking like he hadn't spoken. "I started doubting everything. Doubting my ability to be his dad, doubting my wanting to even be a dad. Doubting if Reagan actually loves me, or if she just loves me *for* her son."

"Are you fucking blind? I've never even seen the two of you together except in pictures, and I know that's not true. Hudson told me she never let *anyone* in before you. Over six years of avoiding people, and you're the one who breaks through that . . . and all of a sudden you think she doesn't love you?"

"Shit, no. I don't know! I told you, it just all came at me at once and I freaked. Don't fucking judge me. Your cunt of a wife refused to let you see her or your kid, and you jumped through hoops to be able to see him. Dropped your career, bought a house, did everything she demanded of you . . . and at the time, you couldn't have even been positive he was your damn kid!"

"Don't fucking spin this around onto me. I'm not the one who just ditched Reagan and Parker! With my situation, I manned up and took responsibility. You're starting to see all the responsibility that comes with being with them, and you *left*."

"I'm not putting it on you, I'm trying to tell you. You handled it your way, even though we all thought you were fucking insane. Now I'm handling this my way. Just because we chose to handle situations differently doesn't mean you can chew me out for this shit."

He huffed and started laughing, but his tone wasn't amused. "You can't begin to compare what I did and what you just did. I knocked my girlfriend up. I wasn't about to let her go through that alone, no matter what was going on between us. You *willingly* went into a relationship with Reagan knowing she had a son and trust issues. Then when it started getting serious and you had a moment of panic, you left. Totally. Different."

Of course they were different. I just needed something . . . anything to try and justify what I'd just done.

"What happened to 'I will never quit,' huh?"

My brow furrowed when I realized what he was saying. It was from part of the Soldier's Creed.

"So you're saying," I began, my voice dark, "that no matter what relationship I got into, if I broke up

Epilogue

Reagan—*June 18, 2011*

LOOKING OVER AT Keegan's fiancée, Erica, I winked and watched as she turned with a smile and began walking away from where I was standing.

"You ready?" Dad asked as he held out his arm for me to take.

With a wide smile, I put my arm through his, bounced up on my toes once, and nodded. "So ready."

"Here we go."

My eyes found Coen's the second we walked into the chapel, and my heart began pounding as I looked at him standing there with Keegan and Parker. I knew I'd waited for this moment my entire life, and I knew I'd found the perfect partner, friend, and lover in Coen—as well as father for Parker.

We still argued instead of talking things out. It still

worked perfectly for us; and not once had either of us walked away until everything was resolved since we got back together. Which usually meant Coen still had to pin me to a hard place when we argued, but in the end, I was thankful for it.

Parker had been beyond excited the night of my birthday when we'd shown up to get him, and hadn't let Coen out of his sight except to sleep and go to school for the next week. Even though he didn't care about the *whys* of Coen's disappearance, Coen had still sat him down and apologized to him while trying to explain all that Parker really needed to know. That Coen had made a mistake, he was back, and he was never leaving again. Three months later, Parker called Coen 'Dad' for the first time as he was falling asleep—and Coen had sat on the end of Parker's bed for ten minutes, fighting back tears.

Keegan made fun of him for that constantly, but it was one of the most beautiful moments I'd ever witnessed between the two of them.

We already had the paperwork ready, and after the wedding, Parker and I were changing our last name to Steele, and Coen was officially adopting him. Something Parker told anyone who gave him two minutes of their time.

When we got to the front, my dad kissed my cheek and handed me off to Coen.

A slow smile pulled at my lips as I stepped up to him, and I studied his dark eyes as they gave away all I needed to know. He was ready for our forever.

"We're—" the pastor began.

"Dad!" Parker whispered.

Coen grinned and looked behind him. "Yeah, bud?"

Everyone sitting in the church began laughing as Parker stepped closer and stood on his toes. "Tell Mom she looks pretty."

"Got it." Looking back at me, Coen's dark eyes brightened as his gaze bounced over my face. "You look beautiful," he said breathlessly.

I squeezed his hand. "Not so bad yourself, Steele."

"You can get married now," Parker declared, and I couldn't help but laugh.

Reaching behind him, Coen put his hand on Parker's back and moved him so he was standing between us. Grabbing his right hand, Coen watched until I grabbed Parker's left hand before looking back over at the pastor.

"Now we're ready."

The End

Keep reading for an early peek at
Molly McAdams's next book

SHARING YOU

The story of Coen's friend Brody.

had in men, and you will *never* know how sorry I am for ever walking away from the two of you."

Slowly wrapping an arm around my waist, he closed the little distance between us and rested his bent head against the side of mine so his nose brushed against the curve of my neck. My body slowly trembled from forcing myself to not grip his hand in mine, but I knew I was slowly losing the battle. He had no idea what his touch and words were doing to me, or maybe he did.

"I am losing my mind without you. I would choose having flashbacks of that mission . . . every night for the rest of my life in a heartbeat if it meant I could have you two for the rest of our forever. A night of not remembering is heaven, but that"—he pointed to the picture of the three of us—"is my peace. You and Parker are my peace. You're my life. My family. I can't live without you, please don't ask me to keep doing it."

I stood there trembling and staring at the picture in front of me for long minutes before I realized I couldn't see it through the tears anymore. Dropping my head, I shook it back and forth as I fought with myself. I was terrified. He'd hurt us, he could do it again. But I was right there with him, I wasn't sure we could live without him. I hadn't felt this whole since the last time I'd set foot in this building, and everything in me was screaming to stop running from him.

With a tortured breath out, his arm slowly left my waist. "I'm sorry, Reagan," he whispered before I heard his footsteps retreat from me.

The war with myself reached deafening levels as he got farther away from me, and it wasn't until I heard the door shut to his studio, did I finally turn from the spot I'd been standing in. Before I could even run after him, I froze in place again and my eyes widened as I saw the backs of the canvases. Down the entire left row was a word on every canvas: IT'S BE-CAUSE OF YOU THAT I STOPPED HIDING FROM MY DEMONS THANK YOU.

And it was then I understood all of it. Starting with the pictures of Coen hiding his eyes or face, changing into the ones of us together where there was no longer anything for him to hide behind, to him baring his soul to tell me more than I'd ever expected him to.

I took off running for the front door, and flung it open. Keegan and Erica were standing against Keegan's truck looking to my left; and when I followed their gazes, I found Coen walking away and running his hands over his face.

I tried calling out his name, but nothing came out as I ran after him. He must have heard my approach, because he turned just in time for me to launch myself at him. He staggered back a step before steadying himself as I wrapped my legs around his waist and pressed my lips firmly to his.

When I finally pulled back, I found his dark eyes filled with tears, and if he hadn't been holding me, the sight would have brought me to my knees. "We can't live without you. I'm sorry I tried to hurt you, I'm so sorry for everything I—"

A Note from the Author

For a look at the pictures from the canvases in the studio, go to:

www.mollysmcadams.com/capturing-peace-photos

Prologue

Kamryn—Sept. 2, 2014

THE SOUND OF three familiar, masculine laughs stopped my retreat to my room and I quietly tiptoed back toward the study. *What are Charles and his dad doing here?* I peeked through the door they had left cracked and was thankful for the darkened hallway. I knew from experience they wouldn't see me unless they were actively searching, and since all of them were huddled around a far table with drinks in their hands, I figured I was fine.

I pulled my cell out of my pocket and glanced at the time before dimming the screen again. Charles wasn't supposed to pick me up for another four hours, and we'd *just* had brunch with his family. Couldn't he go away for a while?

Charles. Good God what had he even changed

into? He had brown loafers—no socks—khaki shorts, and a dark pink polo on. And, yeah, the collar was popped. His dark blond hair had that I-just-got-out-of-bed look, but I'd had the unfortunate pleasure of watching him spend twenty-five minutes to make it look that way this morning, so it lost its appeal.

I'd been dating Charles York since our junior year of high school, and it was safe to say that over the last six years, I'd really come to loathe him. His clothes, his too-perfect bleached smile, his fake tan, his laugh that had to be louder than everyone else's in the room, the fact that he was the *third* Charles York, his signature silver BMW that he upgraded for a new one every two years like it was a cell phone or something. And this was probably worst of all: that he was so close with my dad that he was having drinks with him on his own time.

I'm sure most girls dreamt of a man who their parents would absolutely adore, but my parents hadn't exactly given me a choice when it came to Charles. I had to date him. It was a match made in "Kentucky Derby Heaven," as my mother liked to say. And, no, I'm not joking. Both our families were from the Brighton Country Club neighborhood in Lexington, and every year for the last fifteen years, either Charles's or my family had had a horse win the Kentucky Derby. Our parents were always talking about combining our stables, and I was beginning to think I'd already been sold off to the York family to make this happen.

Why not just break up with him and tell my parents to shove it? Uh, yeah . . . not so easy in my family. I was a Cunningham; in the racing world, we were pretty much royalty. My parents were Bruce and Charlotte, and as the only daughter of the perfect power couple, I was expected to be perfect as well. Perfect hair, perfect clothes, and a perfectly planned life.

The only thing I'd ever done for myself was go to culinary and then pastry school; and it'd been a huge to-do in our house. The only people who had supported me were our maid, Barbara, and surprisingly, Charles. I'd been so taken aback and grateful—since he'd gotten my parents to finally agree to it—that it'd been the only time I'd ever called him by his preferred name, 'Chad.' He hated the name 'Charles,' and I think that is why I refused to call him anything else.

Charles said my name and I leaned closer to the door in time to catch whatever his dad was saying.

"You're sure she'll say yes? I don't know what's going on with that girl of yours, Bruce, but she's seemed rather . . . hesitant lately."

Say yes to what?

"I'm sure of it, she knows her place. She knows how important this merger is."

"I don't know—" Chuck, Charles's father, began.

"Dad, stop. She'll marry me. Like Bruce said, she knows her place; and thank God for that. The sooner she gets off this pipe dream of owning a bakery, the better."

Dad's eyebrows shot up. "That's surprising, seeing

as you're the only one who encouraged Kamryn to go to those food schools."

Charles laughed and took a sip of his drink. "No offense to your home and wife, Bruce, but I want a wife who knows her place in my home as well as by my side."

Chuck and Dad both chuckled. I continued to stand there with my jaw on the floor.

"Charlotte's great for business and public outings," Charles continued "—don't get me wrong—but that woman couldn't cook if her life depended on—"

Dad cut him off. "Which, of course, means Kamryn couldn't cook before she went to those schools."

With the hand holding his scotch glass, Charles pointed at Dad. "Precisely."

"Smart kid you've got there, Chuck." Dad laughed into his glass before taking another sip. "Damn smart kid."

"So you *aren't* letting her open up the bakery? Your mother and I have been worried about your judgment in letting her do this."

"Hell no," Charles laughed. "There's a reason I haven't let her open one yet, I'm just trying to keep her happy until we're married."

"And you'll be proposing tonight?"

My eyes about popped out of my head at my dad's question.

"Yup, gonna push for that whole 'we've been to-gether forever, there's no point in having a long engagement' thing. My guess, end of the year, we'll be married and our families can stop dicking around with this merger."

"Sounds good," Dad said, and the men stood up to shake hands across the table.

I made sure to keep quiet as I quickly backed away from the door and took off for my room. Get married to him? Oh, hell no. I may have stayed with him to keep Mom and Dad happy and off my back for the last six years, but no way in hell was I going into a lifelong commitment with him. And I couldn't believe he would encourage me to go to those schools just so he'd have a wife from the fucking fifties!

"Cook for you?" I hissed as I shut my bedroom door and hurried to the closet. "I'll cook for you." Grabbing a small suitcase, I threw it onto the bed and opened it up. "With rat poison."

I buzzed Barbara before grabbing only my favorite clothes and shoes and tossing everything in there. I was throwing the necessities from my bathroom in a small bag when I heard Barb's voice in my room.

"What can I do for ya, baby girl . . . Kam, honey?"

"Barb!" I apparently still hadn't graduated from hissing. "He's proposing!"

Her eyes were wide as she looked at the too-full suitcase. "I thought we were already expecting that."

"Tonight! And he just told Dad that we would be married by the end of the year, that's barely four months away!"

"Oh, my sweet girl." She smiled sadly and sat on

my bed. "I knew this day was coming, but I'm not ready for it yet."

"Me neither, but Barbara, I can't—I can't keep doing this. Six years with him, and twenty-two years of not being able to live. I *have* to go."

"I know."

"It was one thing to continue dating him while he was away at school and I was trying to save money for this, but it's an entirely different thing to be engaged to him. And you know Mom and Dad won't let me say no!"

"I know," she said again, and there were tears falling down her plump cheeks.

"Barb, don't cry, please don't cry!" God, now I was going to start crying. She'd been our maid since before I was born, she'd taken care of me growing up and she was the reason I'd wanted to go to culinary school. She was also the reason all of this was about to be possible.

Dad refused to pay for the schools, not like I expected him to or would have allowed it, but I'd gotten loans and simultaneously started asking Barb for her help. There was no way for Barb or me to bet on the races without word getting out that we were doing so, and Dad would flip if he knew. I didn't want to use his money for anything, so I'd sold a few things Mom would never notice were missing from my room, and used that money for Barb's brother to start placing bets for me. All the bets started off small, since I hadn't sold anything of much value, and over the last

"Why'd you do that?" he asked gruffly.

"Send him to his room? You're acting weird, and he could tell. I want to figure out what's going on and fix it, and I don't want him around for that."

He put his hands out to the side. "There's nothing to fix, Reagan."

"Even Parker thought you were mad at me, and you've only been here for three minutes. So something happened that you aren't telling me, or you are mad at me. Either way, we're going to talk it out, or argue it out like we always do, and I don't want Parker to see that. So tell me what's going on."

"Oh my God," he groaned into his hands as he ran them down his face. "Nothing is going on."

"I just saw you thirty minutes ago, Coen, and you were fine."

"And I'm still fine!"

"No, you're not!"

He laughed, but it was coated with irritation, and shook his head. "Whatever." Grabbing his keys out of his pocket, he turned and began walking toward the door. "I'm not dealing with this tonight."

"What—you're not dealing with *what* tonight? You're upset, and I want to know why!"

"*This*, your constant nagging. Jesus Christ." He turned to face me. "I barely get in the door and you're already on me trying to figure out if something's wrong."

My jaw dropped. "At your studio, you were the one who hinted at staying tonight, then when Parker asks you, you tell him you don't know and sound like that is the absolute last thing you want to do."

"I'm sorry for not wanting to spend the night, Reagan. I'm sorry I don't want to take Parker to school tomorrow. Sometimes I need a night and a morning to myself. I'm not your husband, he's not my fucking child. It is not my job to take care of you!"

I stumbled back a couple steps and shook my head back and forth. "What?" Hearing a sound off to my right, I turned and saw Parker standing in the hall. "Room," I choked out, and watched until he disappeared.

"I need space. I need to step back so I can just think." His tone had dropped the angry edge, and was now replaced with a heavy exhaustion. "Our entire relationship has moved so fast, and I just—I don't know. But I need time."

My heart dropped, and I couldn't move—couldn't respond. This wasn't happening. My lips parted, but only a short, agonized cry left me. As if someone had dropped a weight on my chest.

"I'm sorry, Reagan," he said quickly as he turned and walked out the door.

I stood there for countless minutes staring at the door as I tried to compose myself. I wouldn't cry. I refused to cry. I'd been protecting us for years from men, and this was why. Because of this possibility. Because Parker had fallen in love with him just as much as I had, like I'd known would happen. Because he ran, just like I'd known he would.

four years they'd multiplied like you wouldn't believe.

I'd paid off the loans before replacing what I'd originally sold from my room first, and then continued to place higher and higher bets. The last race I'd bet on, and won, I'd put down close to six figures. You get the right races, and the right pockets with horses competing; you can make a fortune. And I had.

Barbara and I had spent many nights planning this day, but like she'd said, we weren't expecting it to happen just yet.

"I'm sorry," she said and wiped away some tears. "I'm happy for you, baby girl, really I am. I'm just gonna miss you so much."

"I'll miss you too." I hugged her fiercely and let a few tears escape as she held me. She would be the only person from this entire state I would miss. "As soon as I get to Oregon and get settled, I'll get a phone and call you so you'll have my number."

She nodded and cleared her throat as her arms left my waist to grip my hands. "You can do this, Kamryn. I just know it. You have the money, you have the smarts, you have the talent, and you have the drive. Get away from here, baby girl, and don't come back to this life. This life is its own form of prison."

It was. God it was.

"Do you have everything packed?"

"I do."

"All right." She cleared her throat and her lips quivered as she spoke, "I'm going to call my brother and have him come right over to take you to the train station. I'd just pulled some cookies out of the oven. You go take some and a glass of milk to your daddy. Your mother is at her tennis lesson and then going to a massage, so she won't be back for some time now. By the time you're done sweet-talking your daddy, Ray will be here and I'll have your suitcase and money waiting in his car."

I took a deep breath and stood when she did. "I'll miss you, Barbara, I love you."

"I love you too, baby girl. Go live."

Chapter One

Kamryn—*May 4, 2015*

"KC! Girl, I am definitely going to need some chocolate to get through today."

"Kinlee, seriously?" I huffed as I came through the double doors with trays of cupcakes. "We aren't even open yet. That key I gave you was for emergencies if I wasn't available."

"You're open, I flipped the board for you."

I rolled my eyes and smiled. I'd met Kinlee almost immediately after moving to Jeston, Oregon, and I thanked God every day for that. I'd never had a friend like her, and didn't know how I would get through day-to-day life without her. "Only you, Lee, only you." I handed over a chocolate cupcake with peanut-butter cream-cheese frosting and started stocking my pastry case.

Within two weeks of getting here, I'd bought an SUV, found a condo, and had already leased a small space for what would be my bakery. Over the next two and a half months I was overseeing renovations for KC's Sweet Treats, and that's how I'd met Kinlee. She was two years older than me, shorter than short, with long black hair and a bubbly personality I'd die for. She and her mom had the boutique right next door to me and she'd come by asking if I knew what was going to be put in next to her store. One thing led to another, and I was her new best friend because I could bake. Kinlee could be crude, she could be sweet, and she was loyal to those she cared for. And I absolutely adored every bit of her.

Barbara and I spoke at least once a week when Mom and Dad were both out of the house, and though I missed her like crazy, I didn't regret my decision. I did feel bad for leaving her in that hell storm though. Apparently my parents and Charles's family had gone nuts but ultimately saw it as a chance for more publicity and twisted it to wind up on a few news stations. How? I don't know, and I really don't care. Other than talking with Barbara, I didn't pay attention to anything that had to do with racing or Kentucky. My life was in Oregon now, and that was all I cared to focus on.

And I loved it here. This city of roughly fifteen thousand people had an old-time small-town charm to it, and I wondered how it'd taken me twenty-two years to get here. There was no doubt in my mind: I belonged here.

The best part? No one had a clue who I was.

The minute I'd gotten here and checked into a hotel, I'd found a salon, chopped fourteen inches off my hair and dyed my golden locks a rich brown. Even with the fourteen inches gone, my hair still brushed the tops of my shoulders, and with the thick, black-framed glasses I bought at a drugstore, I looked like a new person. And I couldn't be happier.

"Oh my God, heaven!" Kinlee groaned and hopped onto the counter near the register, "Kace, tell me how you aren't fat yet?"

I laughed, "Probably the same way you aren't."

"You mean you're having wild-animal sex twenty-four seven? I was wondering why you wouldn't let us set you up with anyone! You've been holding out on me, haven't you?"

"Oh God, okay definitely not the same way as you. Ew, Kinlee, all I'm going to be able to think about when I see Jace is you two having wild sex."

"Say that again!"

I froze with my arm inside the pastry case. "Uh, all I'm going—"

"No, no. The last few words." She leaned close and stared at my mouth as I ran over everything I'd said.

"Having wild sex?"

"*Wald*? For real, where are you from?"

I blew out a heavy breath and shook my head as I smirked at my case. "Just not from here." I tried to tame my *accent*—that I didn't know I'd had until I moved here—as much as possible around Kinlee.

She and her husband, Jace, were always trying to figure out where I'd moved from, but them finding out meant them wanting to know why I was here at all. And I wasn't ready for that.

"One of these days, Kace, I will get it out of you." She took another bite of cupcake and moaned. "This is better than *wald* sex with Jace."

"Okay, your husband is hot and all, don't get me wrong, but I really don't want to be thinking about him like that."

"Just saying." She held her hands up. "You were the one that asked."

"Uh, no. No I didn't. And back to your original question: I run most mornings. Not all of us can get away with having crazy hot sex to not get fat, especially when we're not having sex at all."

She shoved the last bit of cupcake in her mouth and spoke through the bite. "KC, I have been trying to set you up for the last seven months! It's not my fault you refuse to go on a date with anyone. You're twenty-three, time to go on a date, woman!"

"Can I remind you that the last guy you tried to set me up with was shorter than me?"

It's not like I'm an Amazon or anything, I'm five-seven, but I do love heels. Just another reason why I couldn't stand Charles, he was one inch taller than me so heels were a no go. Of course I wore heels whenever he wasn't around, but he made me carry flats with me just in case he showed up anywhere I was. There are

I huffed and gritted my teeth. "Olivia, where did you get the furniture and how much did it cost?"

"Do you not like it?"

"That's not what I said, please answer my question." Oh my God, I could only play this game with her so many times before I snapped. And I only had about another two minutes before I lost my calm tone.

"How could you not like it?" Tears instantly fell to her cheeks and I bit back a groan. "I bought them for you, it was only seven grand."

Seven—*seven* grand. *Only* seven grand. "Olivia, where did you get seven grand?" *Please God, please say from your father.*

She sniffed and swiped at her eyes. "You just had five thousand sitting in the savings account, I had to do something with it!"

"Olivia! Are you—are you—damn it! You pulled this shit *again*?"

Her tears kept falling but she stopped sniffling. "How dare you! I did this for you!"

"Every time, Liv, every time I start saving money you go and blow it on something we don't need! And now this time you spent an extra two thousand? I have to pay the mortgage in a week."

"It was a gift, you could at least say thank you! Every time I buy something you get upset, at least I'm *giving* you something, all you've ever done is *take* from me."

With that, she turned and stormed down the hall to her bedroom, leaving me crushed, aching, and once again so damn tired of this. I rubbed my chest where the constant dull ache was now stabbing and fell into one of the kitchen table chairs.

Not more than ten minutes later she was back and bouncing through the kitchen. "Hey, babe! What do you want for dinner?"

I wasn't even surprised by this anymore; I'd just been waiting until she came back. "It's after midnight, Liv, I'm not really hungry."

"Did you already eat dinner? I'll heat some of this up," she murmured the last part to herself as she continued to pull take-out boxes out of the fridge.

"Yeah, earlier tonight."

"Oh." She slammed the fridge door shut and turned to look at me. "All right, I get it. I can't have kids so I'm not good enough to heat up food for you. Yeah, fine, Brody. Feed your damn self."

And here she goes again.

My wife hadn't always been like this—and despite how it seems, she's not crazy—and our relationship hadn't been like this either. We'd been high-school sweethearts, and then I'd left for the army right after we graduated, and everything changed. I came back home to visit after a deployment, and though we had stayed together, Liv and I weren't close anymore. I knew why she'd stayed with me, but I hadn't cared either way: She was someone to come back to when I visited my family.

Her parents hated me, and they let me know it every time they saw me. I wasn't good enough for their daughter because I wasn't going to college and didn't come from money like they had. My family wasn't

"I'm so sorry!" She burst into tears and crumpled to the floor.

Aw hell. I hopped out of my bed and went over to her. Sliding down until I was sitting up against the wall, I pulled her onto my lap. "It's okay, you just have to stop spending our money like that."

"B-but the c-couch we had w-was three years old!"

"I know, and it was still a perfectly good couch," I crooned softly. "Just because your parents can refurnish their entire house every few years, doesn't mean we can, all right?"

She nodded vigorously. "I just—I just needed something to do."

I took a deep breath in and scrunched my face together as I prepared for what might happen next. I knew this could turn out bad again, but I had to try. "Maybe we should get a dog."

"A dog? A damn *dog*? No! You can't just give me a dog and make it all better, Brody!" She scrambled off my lap and sprinted down the hall, heading for her side of the house.

Yes, I said *her* side of the house. I normally don't even see her because she prefers to spend her days at her parents' house unless she's in a mood like the one tonight. It usually lasts a week, as this one has, and we go through every emotion possible about fifteen times a day. I try to be patient with her because I know I'm the reason she's like this, but after four and a half years of this constant happy-depressed-flirty-pissed-horny-sweet-flat-out-bitch roller coaster, I feel like I'm losing my damn mind. And what's worse? As soon as we're in public she's normal Liv—not the Liv I fell in love with in high school, but the one who's confident in herself and her parents' money, and the one who will eat you alive if you cross her.

Her door slammed shut and I stood to stumble over to my bed, thankful again that I was able to buy a big enough house that we could have our own spaces. We'd been married for almost six years, and I could count on one hand the number of times we'd had sex in those years. We hadn't even slept in the same bed since a month after I got back from the army.

As I tried to get comfortable enough to go back to sleep, I rubbed at the ache in my chest and prayed the nightmares stayed away.

only so many flats you can wear before you want to find all the flats in the world and burn them.

"I only know so many single men!"

"This barbecue tomorrow, you aren't going to try . . ." I trailed off when I noticed her looking away. "Kinlee!"

"I didn't invite them! Swear to God I didn't invite them this time. The guys on Jace's shift from the department are all gonna be there, and most of them are single, not my fault."

Oh Lord, single firemen.

"But it won't just be the guys from the department, there will be other people, some couples from the neighborhood, all people you've met before."

I nodded and shut the pastry-case doors "All right, well you know I'll be there, not like I have anything else to do on a Sunday. Want me to bring something?" I don't know why I even bothered asking anymore, it's not like I'd show up without something anyway.

"Cookies, cupcakes, whatever you want." She leaned back and blew an air kiss before jumping off the counter. "Jeez, KC, I know you needed help taste testing and all—what, with your lovely faces you make—but you've really got to stop keeping me from opening the store. You're bad for my hips and business."

"My faces when I eat sweets are a secret, Lee! Only you know about them!"

With a wink and a saucy smile, she was gone.

Well, she was the only one in Oregon who knew about them. I was teased relentlessly in pastry school for the faces I'd make whenever we tried our dishes, and Barb used to give a big belly laugh every time as well. Charles wouldn't let me eat sweets in public *because* of those expressions, but he sure seemed to like them when we were alone. I shivered thinking about Charles and was glad that for eight months now I hadn't had to pretend to not be swallowing back bile every time he kissed or touched me. I took a quick glance at the front of my bakery and smiled to myself before going to the back. For the first time in my life, I was exactly where I wanted to be.

Brody—*May 4, 2015*

"OLIVIA!" *What the fuck is all this?*

"Hmm?"

"Liv, come here."

"What?" she snapped when she got into the living room.

I took a deep, calming breath and planted a smile on my face. "What's all this?"

"It's called furniture, Brody." Her eyebrows rose. "You know, you sit on the couches, put drinks on the coffee table, put your feet up on the ottoman . . ."

"Cute, Liv, real cute. Where did it come from?"

"The furniture store," she said slowly like she was talking to a child.

Chapter One

Rachel

"CANDICE, YOU NEED to focus. You have got to pass this final or they aren't going to let you coach this summer."

She snorted and her eyes went wide as she leaned even closer to the mirror and tried to re-create her snort. "Oh my God! Why didn't you tell me how ugly I look when I do that!?"

I face-planted into the pillow and mumbled, "Oh dear Lord, this isn't happening." Lifting my head, I sent her a weak glare. "Snorts aren't meant to be cute. Otherwise they wouldn't be called something as awkward as 'snort.'"

"But my—"

"Final, Candice. You need to study for your final."

"I'm waiting on you," she said in a singsong voice. "You're supposed to be quizzing me."

I loved Candice. I really did. Even though I currently wanted to wring her neck. She wasn't just my best friend; she was like a sister to me and was the closest thing to family I had left. On the first day of kindergarten, a boy with glasses pushed me down on the playground. While he was still laughing at me, Candice grabbed his glasses and smashed them on the ground. That's playground love. And since then we've never spent more than a handful of days apart.

By the time we started thinking about college, it was just assumed we would go away together. But then my parents died right before my senior year of high school started, and nothing seemed to matter anymore. They had gone on a weekend getaway with two partners from my dad's law firm and their wives and were on their way home when the company jet's engine failed and went down near Shaver Lake.

Candice's family took me in without a second thought since the only relatives I had lived across the country and I hardly knew them; if it weren't for them I don't know how I would have made it through that time. They made sure I continued going to school, kept my grades up, and attempted to live as normal a life as possible. I no longer cared about graduating or going away to college, but because of them, I followed through with my plans of getting away and making my own life. I would forever be grateful to the Jenkins family.

I applied to every college Candice did and let her decide where we were going. She'd been a cheerleader for as long as I could remember, so it shouldn't have

"You never answered my question."

"What question?"

"Are you going to go on a date with Blake?"

I sighed and fell into the chair at my desk. "One, he's your *cousin*. Two, he works for UT now; that's just . . . kinda weird. Three, no."

"It's not like he's your professor! He isn't even a professor, period. And do you realize that if you marry him, we'll actually be family?"

"Marry? Candice— Wait . . . how do you even jump from me going on a date with him to marrying him? I'm not going to marry your cousin; sorry. And I don't care if he's a professor or not, it doesn't change the fact that he works for the school. Besides, he's not even my type."

"Not your type?" she said, deadpan, and one perfect blond eyebrow shot straight up. "I seem to remember you having the *biggest* crush on him when we were growing up. And I know he's family, but I can still say that he's gorgeous. I'm pretty sure he's everyone's type."

I had to agree with her on that. Blake West was tall, blond, and blue eyed and had a body like a god's. One of these days he was going to show up on a Calvin Klein billboard. "I had a crush on him when we were thirteen. That was eight years ago."

"But you had a crush on him for years. Years. You were devastated when he moved away."

"And like I said, I was thirteen. I was ridiculous."

Blake was five years older than Candice and me,

but even so, all of my childhood memories included him. He was always at Candice's house to hang out with her older brother, Eli, and we followed them everywhere. I'd viewed both Eli and Blake as awesome older brothers until the day Blake saved my life.

Okay, that's a little dramatic. He didn't actually save my life.

I was nine at the time; we'd been playing on a rope swing and jumping into a little lake not far from our houses. When I'd gone to jump, my foot slipped into the foot hole and I ended up swinging back toward land headfirst, screaming the whole way. Blake was standing on the bank and caught me, swinging me into his arms before I could make the trip back toward the water.

In that moment, he became my hero, and I fell in love. Or at least my nine-year-old version of love. My infatuation with him grew over the next few years, but he never saw me as anything other than his "little cousin's best friend." I'm sure if I'd been older, that would have been a blow to my ego, but I just kept following him around like I'd always done. When he graduated from high school, he immediately joined the air force and moved away from me. I remember throwing a few "my life is over" fits to Candice, but then I got boobs and hips and the other boys my age started noticing me. And then it was something along the lines of, "Blake who?"

He'd been out of the air force for four years now and had pretty much been off the grid until last fall, when he'd moved to Austin and started working at UT. Candice had flipped out over having her cousin near her again. And I'd just straight flipped out. But then I saw him. He looked like freakin' Adonis standing there in his godlike, too-beautiful-for-his-own-good glory. Every straight female within a mile radius seemed to flock to him, and he loved every second of it.

That is why I refused to go on a date with him.

"Rachel," Candice snapped.

I turned my wide gaze to her.

"Did you even hear me?"

"Not unless we're done talking about Blake."

"We are if you've decided to say yes to him."

I rolled my eyes. "Why is it so important to you if I go on a date with him or not?"

"Because he's been asking you out all year! He's my cousin and you're my best friend and I love you both and I want to see you two together."

"Well, I'm pretty sure you and Blake are the only two who feel that way. I have absolutely no desire to date a guy who has women literally hanging on him all the time." *Stupid air force, turning him into sex on a stick.*

Suddenly she was sporting her signature pouty face. "Rach? How much do you love me?"

"Nope. No, I'm not going."

"Are you saying you don't love me?" I was already shaking my head to say no when she turned on the puppy eyes and continued. "So will you please do this for me? Pleeeeaaasse? I thought you were my best friend."

I can't even believe we're doing this right now! "If I go on *one* date with him, will you drop this forever?"

She squeaked and did a happy clap. "Thank you, I love you, you're the best!"

"I didn't say I would, I said *if.*"

"But I know you'll go."

"He works for the school!" I whined, going back to my original argument. Even though he wasn't a professor at UT, he did work there as a personal trainer and helped out in the athletics department. Since I was majoring in athletic training and Candice in kinesiology and health ed, we saw him almost daily in classroom-type settings. That just . . . didn't sit right with me.

"Rachel." She twisted back around to face me. "Seriously, that is getting old. He already checked it out and it's a nonissue. Stop acting like you don't want to date him."

"I don't! Who wants to date a man-whore?"

"He isn't a—well . . . eh." She made a face. "Well, yeah."

"Exactly!" Blake was rumored to be screwing most of the females he trained as well as . . . well . . . he was rumored to be screwing pretty much any female he passed. Whether the rumors were true or not was up for debate. But seeing as he didn't try to squash them and the horde of bimbos was never far from him, I was leaning toward their being true.

"You haven't dated anyone since Daniel. You need to get back out there."

"Yes I have. Candi, just because I'm not constantly seen with a guy, like you are, doesn't mean I don't date."

I had gotten kind of serious with Daniel at the beginning of our second year at UT. But apparently six months was too long to make him wait to have sex and he ended up cheating on me. I found out two days after I'd given him my virginity.

Asshole.

After him I'd gone out with a few guys, but they didn't last much longer than a date or two and an "I'll call you later." Not that there was anything wrong with those guys, I was just more interested in being done with school and Texas than getting my "MRS degree" or risking catching a disease.

I sighed to myself and headed toward our door.

"Are you going to find Blake?!" Candice was bouncing in her seat and her face was all lit up like a kid's on Christmas morning.

"What—Candice, no. It's after midnight! I'm just done talking about this. I'm going to wash my face so I can go to sleep. And I'm not gonna hunt him down either; *if* he asks me out again, then I'll say yes." I grabbed my face wash and was reaching for the knob when someone knocked on the door. I don't know who I was expecting it to be, but I wouldn't have thought Blake West would be the one standing there in all his cocky glory. From the look on his face, there was no doubting he'd heard part, if not all, of our conversation. What the eff was he doing in our dorm?

He pulled one long-stemmed red rose—that was unexpected—from behind his back and looked over my shoulder, and his cocky expression went completely serious. "Hey, Candi. Do you mind if I steal Rachel for a few minutes?"

I turned around to look at her and she was grinning like the Cheshire Cat. *Traitor.* I looked back at Blake and he let out a short laugh at my question-mark expression.

"That is, unless you're busy or don't want to. It looks like you were headed somewhere." He looked pointedly at the hand that wasn't holding on to the door.

It took me a few seconds to look down at my hand and realize he was looking at my face wash. "Oh . . . um, not. No. I mean. Busy. Not busy. I'm not busy." *Wow, that was brilliant.*

Blake's lips twitched and his head fell down and to the side to hide the grin he was failing at keeping back.

Trying not to continue looking like a complete idiot, I took a deep breath in and actually thought about my next question two different times before asking it. Okay, fine, I thought about it four times. "So, what can I do for you?" Yeah, I know. Now you understand why that required a lot of thought.

"I was wondering if I could talk to you for a few minutes."

"Uh, you do realize it's almost one in the morning, right?"

His head lifted and he looked sheepish. That look on this man was so different from anything I'd ever seen, and I almost didn't know how to respond to it. "Yeah, sorry. I think I fought with myself for so long on whether or not I should actually come up here and talk to you, it got a lot later than I realized." He jerked the rose up in front of him like he'd just remembered it was there. "This is for you, by the way."

"And here I was thinking you just walk around holding roses all the time." I awkwardly took the rose from him, looked at it for a few seconds, then let it hang from the tips of my fingers. "So, Blake . . ." I trailed off and searched his eyes for a second before he took a step back.

"Can I talk to you out here for just a minute? I promise I won't keep you long."

Yeah, well, the fact that I've turned you down for the amount of time it takes to make a baby and now you're standing at my dorm room door at one in the morning is kind of creepy. But of course we have history, you're incredibly hot now, and I'm thinking about as clearly as Candice does. So, sure. Why the hell not? I followed him out into the hall and shut the door behind us but stayed pressed up against it.

"Rachel . . ." He ran a nervous hand through his hair and paused for a second, as if trying to figure out what to say. "The school year is about to end and you'll be going back to Cali over the summer. I feel like I'm about to miss any chance with you I may have. And I don't want to. I know you liked me when we were growing up. But, Rach, you were way too young back then."

"I'm still five years younger; that hasn't changed."

He smirked. "You and I both know a relationship between a thirteen-year-old and eighteen-year-old, and a twenty-one- and twenty-six-year-old are completely different."

So? That doesn't help my argument right now. "Well, you and I have both changed over the last eight years. Feelings change—"

"Yes." He cut me off and his blue eyes darkened as he gave me a once-over. "They do."

I hated that my body was responding to his look. But honestly, I think it'd have been impossible for anyone not to respond to him. Like I said. Adonis. "Uh, Blake. Up here." He smiled wryly, and dear Lord, that smile was way too perfect. "Look, honestly? I have an issue with the fact that you're constantly surrounded by very eager and willing females. It's not like I'd put some claim on you if we went on a couple dates, but you ask me out *while* these girls are touching you and drooling all over you. It's insulting that you would ask me out while your next lay is already practically stripping for you."

His expression darkened and he tilted his head to the side. "You think I'm fucking them like everyone else?"

Ah, frick. Um, yes? "If you are, then that's your business. I shouldn't have said that, I'm sorry. But whether you are or not, you don't even attempt to push them away. Since you moved here, I've never seen you with less than two women touching you. You don't find that weird?" Was I *really* the only person who found this odd?

Suddenly pushing off the wall he'd been leaning against, he took the two steps toward me and I tried to mold myself to the door. A heart-stopping smile and bright blue eyes now replaced his darkened features as he completely invaded my personal space. If he weren't so damn beautiful I'd have karate-chopped him and reminded him of personal bubbles. Or gone all Stuart from *MADtv* on him and told him he was a stranger and to stay away from my danger. Instead, I tried to control my breathing and swallow through the dryness in my mouth.

"No, Rachel. What I find weird is that you don't seem to realize that I don't even notice those other women or what they're doing because all I see is you. I look forward to seeing you every day. I don't think you realize you are the best part of my weekdays. I moved here for this job before I even knew you and Candice were going to school here, and seeing you again for the first time in years—God, Rachel, you were so beautiful and I had no idea that it was you. You literally stopped me in my tracks and I couldn't do anything but watch you.

"And you have this way about you that draws people to you . . . always have. It has nothing to do with how devastatingly beautiful you are—though that doesn't hurt . . ." He smirked and searched my face. "But you have this personality that is rare. And it bursts from you. You're sweet and caring, you're genuinely happy, and it makes people around you happy. And you have a smile and laugh that is contagious."

Only men like Blake West could get away with saying things like that and still have my heart racing instead of making me laugh in their faces.

"You're not like other women. Even though these are the years for it, you don't seem like the type of girl to just have flings, and I can assure you, that's not what I'm into, nor what I'm looking for with you. So I don't see those other women; all I'm seeing is you. Do you understand that now?"

Holy shit. He was serious?

"Rachel?"

I nodded and he smiled.

"So, will you please let me take you out this weekend?"

For the first time since he'd come back into my life, he actually looked unsure of himself. I was still in complete shock, but I somehow managed to nod again and mumble, "Sure, where do you want to go?"

He smiled wide and exhaled in relief. "It's a surprise."

I frowned. How did he have a surprise planned if he hadn't even known I was going to say yes? "And by 'surprise,' do you mean you have no clue?"

"No, it's just a surprise."

I started to turn into Candice and whine that I wouldn't know what to wear but was interrupted by my own huge yawn, which made me sound more like Chewbacca. I covered as much of my face as possible with the hand that wasn't holding the rose and laughed awkwardly. "Oh my word, that's embarrassing."

His laugh was deep and rich. "It's late and I stopped you from going to sleep. If for some reason I don't see you for the rest of the week, I'll pick you up at seven on Friday. That sound all right?"

"That sounds perfect. I'll see you then, and, uh, thanks for my rose." Before he could say anything else, I turned the doorknob, gave him a small smile, backed up into the room, and shut the door in his still-smirking face. "Holy hell," I whispered, and let my forehead fall against the door.

"Tell. Me. *Everything!*" Candice practically shrieked, and I turned to narrow my eyes at her.

Like she hadn't been listening.

"We're going on a date Friday. That's about it."

"That is *so* not all that was said, Rachel! Ohmigod, did you swoon when he said all he's seeing is you?"

"Swoon, Candice? Really? This isn't one of your romance novels." And yeah . . . I did kind of swoon. "And that's exactly why I'm not telling you. You eavesdrop anyway, so what's the point in going over it all again?"

"Because I want details of how he looked at you and how you reacted to him."

Oh dear God, this was going to be a long night.

WHY BLAKE THOUGHT we wouldn't see each other the rest of the week was beyond me, because sure enough he was the first person I saw when I walked into the athletic center the next afternoon. And surprise, surprise . . . he only had four girls around him that day. That wasn't including the one he was stretching out on the ground.

Candice's constant talking faded out as I watched him explaining why he was stretching those particular muscles. But I knew the girl wasn't paying attention; all she could care about was that he was practically in between her legs.

The girl on the ground said something I couldn't hear, and the runway-beautiful, mocha-skinned girl standing closest to me practically purred as she reached for his forearm, "Well, that's just because Blake's so good with his . . . *hands.*" The other four girls started giggling and I wanted to gag.

Blake's head shot up and I realized I must have actually gagged out loud. *Whoops.* Our eyes locked for a few seconds before he quickly looked at the girls surrounding him and his position with the one on the floor. When he looked back at me, his blue eyes were pleading, but I just shook my head and walked off toward the back to get my out-of-the-classroom part of my course over with.

"Hey." Candice nudged me. "Don't get upset about that. They aren't the ones who have a date with him on Friday."

"I'm not upset about that." I was upset about the fact that *that* pissed me off. What, did I expect him to change overnight just because we were going to go on one date? Or did his words last night really have me thinking I'd imagined his robot bimbo herd all year? And sheesh, why did I care at all? I didn't even want to go on a date with him! Not really . . .

An hour and a half later, I'd successfully avoided his gaze, which I could feel like a laser on my back. But when I turned to put some equipment away, he was right there and there was no way I could avoid Blake in all his real-life Calvin Klein model–ness.

"You're mad," he said, and began taking the equipment out of my arms and putting it in the closet.

"Um . . . not? And I can put this away myself."

"Rachel, I told you. I only see you."

"Yeah, no, I heard you." As soon as everything was put up, I turned away, only to quickly turn back around and face him. "Look, Blake, I don't think Friday is a good idea."

"Why isn't it?"

"Well, it's—you know . . . it's just not. So thank you for your offer. But once again, and hopefully for the last time, I'm not going to go on a date with you. If you ever move back to California, I really hope this doesn't make family dinners awkward."

The corners of his lips turned up slightly. "All right. You done for the day?"

This was the first rejection he'd taken well, and it threw me off for a moment. "Um, yes?"

"Let's go then."

"Whoa, wait. Go where? Its Wednesday, not Friday. And I said no anyway."

"You said no to a date with me. The date was on Friday. So we aren't going on a date. We're just going to go walk, hang out, whatever you want. But it's not a date." He stepped close enough that we were sharing the same air and his voice got low and husky. "If you want to call it something, we can call it exercising or seeing Austin. You can hardly count that as a date, Rach."

I was momentarily stunned by the effect his voice and blue eyes had on me. "Um . . ." I blinked rapidly and looked down to clear my head. "I've lived here almost three years, I don't need to see the sights."

"Perfect, I don't get out much other than to come to work, so I do. You can be my tour guide."

"Blake—"

"Come on, Rachel."

Not giving me an option, he grabbed on to my arm and began towing me out of the building. I caught sight of Candice and she waved excitedly as she watched us leave.

Why was she smiling? I sure as hell wasn't smiling, and Blake was practically dragging me away! He could have been hauling me off to slaughter me and leave my remains on a pig farm for all she knew, and Candice was just going to sit there and wave like a lunatic? Playground. Love. Over. Best-friend card officially revoked.

As soon as we were outside, I yanked my arm free and continued to follow Blake as he made his way off campus. Well, at least he was right about one thing: I couldn't count this as a date. No way would I have worn baggy sweats cut off at my calves and a tight tank on a date.

"Are you still mad?"

I glanced up to see his stupid smirk, which I kind of hated right now. "Why would I be mad? I was just dragged out of a building to go *walk* with a guy I turned down for a date."

His smirk turned into a full-blown smile. "Still mad," he said, and looked ahead. "Although I always did find your temper adorable, let me know when you're not."

Thirty minutes later I was getting tired of following him around. Tour guide my nonexistent ass. He wasn't looking at anything. He was walking with a purpose and hadn't looked back at me since he'd asked if I was mad.

"So, this has been awesome and all. Are you going to tell me where we're going now?"

"Are you going to tell me what you're mad about?"

"I'm not mad!"

He slowed his pace so he was directly next to me and I was surprised to see him looking at me completely seriously. "Yes you are, Rach. If you didn't want to go on the date on Friday, you would have never agreed, and you wouldn't be following me right now." I opened my mouth but he cut me off. "You would have gone back to your dorm and you know it. I was two steps ahead of you the entire time; you could have turned back if you were really mad at me."

"You didn't even give me an option to say no!" He raised an eyebrow and I huffed, "All right. Fine. Maybe I am mad."

"And you're mad at me."

"Yeah, Blake, I am."

"But not because I pulled you out of the building."

Oh my word, he was so infuriating! "Uh, yeah, I'm pretty sure that's why I'm mad. Are you going to start telling me I'm not hungry either? Since you all of a sudden seem to know me so well?"

He pulled me to a stop and moved to stand directly in front of me, tipping my head back with his fingers under my chin. "You're mad because of the girls around me when you walked in this afternoon."

"I—"

"And I told you I only see you. I'll tell you that over and over again until you understand that. They mean nothing, nor do I notice anything other than the fact that they talk like they're in middle school."

"I don't care about them the way you think I do. When I saw it, it just reminded me why I never wanted to go on a date with you in the first place. Nothing more, nothing less."

"You're lying, Rachel." I could smell the mint from his gum and feel his breath on my lips, and suddenly I was wondering if I *was* lying. There must have been something in his gum that put me in a daze. "It's fine to admit you were getting jealous. I hate seeing the way Aaron looks at you, and you work with him every day."

I was so not getting jeal— Wait. What?! Aaron's gay. I leaned away from his nearness and started to tell him when I realized we were on top of a bridge surrounded by a bunch of people just standing there looking toward the side like they were waiting for something. I pointed toward the people. "Uh . . . am I missing something?"

Blake looked a little smug as he glanced at his watch, then the sky. "Nope, give it a couple minutes. We got here just in time."

Aaron, his sexuality, and the fact that Blake had gotten jealous over my flaming gay friend completely forgotten, I looked at the sky, then pulled out my phone to check the time. There was nothing special about the time from what I could tell. As for the sky, it was nearly dusk, and although it was beautiful I didn't know why that was anything worth noting either. Glancing at the people and the street around us, I turned and saw the street sign and did a double take. We were on Congress Avenue.

"Oh no. No, no, no, no, no!" I started backing up but ended up against Blake's chest. His arms circled around me, effectively keeping me there. I felt his silent laughter.

"I take it you know about this then. Ever seen it?"

"No, and there's a reason. I'm terrified of—" Just then, close to a million bats took flight from underneath the bridge. A small shriek escaped my lips and I clamped my hands over my mouth, like my sound would attract the bats to me.

There was nothing silent about his next laugh. Blake tightened his arms around me and I leaned into him more. I'd like to say it was purely because my biggest fear was flying out around me, but I'd be lying if I said his musky cologne, strong arms, and chest had nothing to do with it either. This was something I'd wanted for years, and I almost couldn't believe that I was finally there, in his arms.

I continued to watch in utter horror and slight fascination as the stream of bats, which seemed to never end, continued to leave the shelter of the bridge and fly out into the slowly darkening sky.

Minutes later, Blake leaned in and put his lips up against my ear. "Was that really so bad?"

Forcing my hand from my mouth, I exhaled shakily and shook my head. "Not as bad as I'd imagined. Doesn't change the fact that they are ugly and easily the grossest thing I've ever seen."

"But now you can say you've faced one of your fears."

"The biggest."

"See?" He let go of me and started walking again in the direction we'd come from. "You up for a drink?"

I realized I was still shaking so I nodded my head and followed him. "Just one though."

We walked for well over half an hour while Blake tried to re-create my shriek at seeing the bats and I accused him of doing that with every girl so he'd have an excuse to put his arms around her. The air between us was much more relaxed this time as he asked about my life after he'd joined the air force. I told him all about the end of middle school and high school but never once mentioned my parents. I wasn't sure if he knew about them or not, but there was no point in bringing up that hurt. Besides, if he had known, he hadn't even come back for the funeral. Just as we were passing the school, Blake slid his hand down my arm and intertwined our fingers.

"Rachel, why did you finally agree to go out with me?"

When I looked up, I was surprised at his somber expression. I would have expected something a little more taunting. "Do you want me to answer that honestly?"

"I'd appreciate it. I've asked you out for . . . shit. I don't know, nine months now? No matter what I said, your answer was always no. Until last night."

"Well . . ." I looked down at the sidewalk passing beneath our feet.

"You can tell me, it's fine. You never were one to hide your feelings. And your hate for me lately has been a little more than apparent. I'm already expecting the worst."

"I don't hate you. I just don't exactly like you . . . anymore." I squinted up at him and nudged his side with the arm he still had a firm grip on.

He gave a little grunt with a forced smile.

"Um, Candice is always bugging me for turning you down. She said she would stop if I agreed to one date with you." I know, I know, I could have made something up that wasn't so harsh. But I didn't. If I hadn't looked back down, I probably would have missed the pause in his step.

"Figures." We walked for a few more minutes before he paused and turned to me. "I'm not going to make you go out with me."

"You aren't. I said I'd go."

He raised an eyebrow, making it disappear under his shaggy hair. "You also told me earlier today that we weren't going anymore. I'm just letting you know I'll stop. All of it. Asking you all the time, what I did today. And I'll talk to Candice."

"Blake—"

"No, Rach, I should have stopped a long time ago. I'm sorry you felt pressured into it last night. I want you to *want* to go on a date with me. I don't want you to go just so she'll drop it or because you want me to quit asking. Which I will." I couldn't tell if he looked more embarrassed or hurt.

Is it ridiculous that I want to comfort him? "I want to go."

"No, you don't."

Okay, still somewhat true. "I didn't . . . before." *Ugh, who am I kidding. He knows I'm lying anyway.* "Look, I don't know what you want me to say. You can't exactly blame me for not wanting to go out with you." He looked as if I'd slapped him. I hurried on before I could chicken out on the rest. "I mean, come on, Blake, you were rumored to be screwing all these students, coworkers, and faculty. And not once did you try to shut down those rumors. Add to that, the Blake I grew up with is completely gone; now you're usually kind of a douche. Why *would* I want to go out with someone like that?"

"Rumors are going to spread no matter what I do. The more I try to stop them, the guiltier I look. Trust me. As for you thinking I'm a douche . . ." His voice trailed off and he ran a hand through his hair. "Try seeing it from my side. The only girl I've wanted for years now and can't get out of my head no matter what I do repeatedly blows me off like I'm nothing."

Did he say years?

Letting go of my hand, he turned away from me and ran a hand agitatedly through his hair. "Come on, I'll walk you back to your dorm."

"What about drinks?"

"I'm not going to make you do this, Rachel."

"Blake, why can't you just be like this all the time? If how you were growing up, last night, and the last hour was how you always were . . . I probably wouldn't have ever turned you down."

He huffed a sad laugh. "Yeah, well . . . obviously I've already fucked that up."

I watched him begin walking in the direction of the dorms and squeezed my eyes shut as I called after him, "You know, you kinda traumatized me tonight. I feel like you owe me a beer." Peeking through my eyelashes, I saw him stop but not turn around. "And maybe dinner on Friday night?"

When Blake turned to face me, his smile was wide and breathtaking.

About the Author

MOLLY McADAMS grew up in California but now lives in the oh-so-amazing state of Texas with her husband and furry four-legged daughters. Some of her hobbies include hiking, snowboarding, traveling and long walks on the beach . . . which roughly translates to being a homebody with her hubby and dishing out movie quotes. When she's not diving into the world of her characters, she can be found hiding out in her bedroom surrounded by her laptop, cell, Kindle and fighting over the TV remote. She has a weakness for crude-humored movies, fried pickles and loves curling up in a fluffy comforter during a thunderstorm . . . or under one in a bathtub if there are tornados. That way she can pretend they aren't really happening.

Visit www.AuthorTracker.com for exclusive information on your favorite HarperCollins authors.

surprised me when she decided on a university based on the football team and school spirit. And granted, she was given an amazing scholarship. But Texas? Really? She chose the University of Texas at Austin and started buying everything she found in that god-awful burnt-orange color. I wasn't exactly thrilled to be a "Longhorn," but whatever got me away from my hometown was fine by me . . . and I guess the University of Texas accomplished that.

When we first arrived I remember it felt like walking into a sauna, it was so hot and humid; of course the first thing Candice said was, "What am I going to do with my *hair*?!" Her hair had already begun frizzing, and not more than five minutes later she was rocking a fro. We got used to the humidity and crazy weather changes soon enough though, and to my surprise, I *loved* Texas. I had been expecting dirt roads, tumbleweeds, and cowboys—let me tell you, I had never been so happy to be wrong. Downtown Austin's buildings reminded me of Los Angeles, and the city was unbelievably green everywhere and had lakes and rivers perfect for hanging out with friends. Oh, and I'd only seen a couple of cowboys in the almost three years we'd been there, not that I was complaining when I did. I had also worried when we arrived that with Candice's new burnt-orange fetish, people were going to be able to spot us like Asian tourists at Disneyland. Thankfully, the majority of Austin was packed with UT Longhorn gear, and it was common to see a burnt-orange truck on the road.

Now we were a little less than two weeks away from finishing our junior year and I couldn't wait for the time off. Normally we went to California to see Candice's family during the winter and summer breaks, but she was working at a cheer camp for elementary-school girls that summer, so we were getting an apartment that we planned to keep as we finished our senior year.

That is, if we ever got Candice to pass this damn final.

Before I could even ask my first question, Candice gasped loudly. "Oh my God, the pores on my nose are huge."

Grabbing the pillow under me, I launched it at her and failed miserably at hitting anything, including her. At least it got her attention. Her mouth snapped shut, she turned to look at the pillow lying a few feet from her, then she turned around with a huff to walk back to her desk.

Finally. "Okay, what is—".

"So are you ever going to go on a date with Blake?"

"Candice!"

"What?" She shot me an innocent look. "He's been asking you out for a year!"

"This—you need—forget it." I slammed the book shut and rolled off my bed, stretching quickly before going to drop the heavy book on my desk. "Forget it, we'll just see if we can get our deposit on the apartment back. I swear to God, it's like trying to study with a five-year-old."

Want more?
Read on for a peek at Molly McAdams's
New York Times Bestseller

FORGIVING LIES

poor by any means; we'd grown up in a great house in a great neighborhood. But we weren't dripping with money and we didn't belong to the country club that Liv's parents did. So apparently that meant we were trash. Olivia loved that her parents didn't accept me, and I knew that was the only reason we'd stayed together as long as we had. But like I said, I didn't mind.

I had had a year left in the army when my world changed. She'd called me crying, saying she was pregnant. I'd requested emergency leave as soon as we got off the phone and married her the minute I got home. Her parents were furious—hell, so were mine—but no way in hell was I going to let her go through that alone. I couldn't take care of her like her parents did, but I'd take care of them the best I could.

It took a lot of people high up pulling strings, but I'd been able to get us a house on base for as soon as I had to get back. Only thing was, she'd refused to go to base with me. Basically said thanks for marrying her and she was going to stay with her parents until I decided I was done "playing navy." Shit you not. And I wasn't even in the navy.

I couldn't get leave often, but even when I did, she still didn't see me. Didn't even try. When I asked her, she'd said, "What's the point? We're already married."

Yeah. Married and I haven't seen you since two days after the fact.

The only thing she had included me in was the baby. After every appointment she'd sent pictures of the ultrasound, and she'd let me help her pick out a name. I'd gotten the message the minute she went into labor, and received more pictures after he was delivered. The next time I got leave, she'd still refused to see me and wouldn't let me see our son. Instead, I'd stood outside her parents' house and called her only to find out that if I wanted to see either of them, I wouldn't re-enlist and I'd move back to Jeston.

So that's what I did: When it came time to re-enlist, I declined and moved back. Bought us a house, it wasn't much and her dad let me know that all the time, but I'd bought it and that's all that mattered. Once I had it furnished, I called her and she finally let me meet my son for the first time.

"Brody!" Olivia snapped, and I blinked away the memory of best day of my life. She held up her hand momentarily to show she was on the phone before continuing. "Daddy said he'd pay you back for the couches, since obviously with your pay you can't afford what I need to be happy."

My eyes narrowed. It was almost twelve thirty in the morning, and she was calling her dad to talk to him about the damn couches? I rubbed the sharp pain in my chest and pushed away from the table before standing up. "He can keep his money, I don't want it. Good night, Olivia."

"BABY, ARE YOU awake?"

I sat up in my bed less than an hour later and rubbed a hand over my face. "Uh, yeah. What's up, Liv?"

may be amazing. But I thought my girl had been amazing too. I'd admired how strong she was, and how she never wanted help from anyone. How she'd never let anyone into her and her daughter's life before me. How she supported her and her daughter all by herself. It wasn't until push came to shove that everything began unraveling, and I found out everything had been bullshit. An illusion that the four of us— hell, maybe even more—had fallen for."

My body had locked up at some point, and I had to force myself to start breathing again. Keeping my expression blank so he wouldn't realize he'd just explained Reagan perfectly, I stared at him for a bit longer as I tried to block the words he'd just told me, and finally shook my head. "You don't know my girlfriend."

"All right. I'm sorry, you're right, I don't. I just . . . when you said she was your girlfriend, it was like déjà vu, and I wish there'd been someone to warn me. So, I had to at least give you something to think about. I told you, she might be amazing. That was just my experience, and I felt like I needed to warn you or something. Sorry for overstepping my bounds."

"Let's just finish this shoot, yeah?" I walked over to grab my camera, and no matter how hard I tried not to think about it . . . I couldn't stop.

His story, and thoughts of what Saco was currently going through, flooded my mind. One with an ex-girlfriend who matched mine. One with a wife who had succeeded in trapping him in a marriage by getting pregnant. I'd never once worn a condom with Reagan. Even though she'd avoided men, she'd been on the pill ever since Parker was born.

Or, that's what she'd told me.

Now that I thought about it. That didn't make sense.

No . . . no. I knew Reagan. I *knew* her. I loved her. I loved Parker.

But then, why would she suddenly let in a guy after so many years of avoiding them? And a guy like me? I was damaged. I had demons. I was constantly trying to figure out what I'd done to deserve someone like her . . . and now us together made even less sense. Had I seemed like an easy target? Someone who would easily believe her story?

Pressing my hand against my forehead, I willed all this bullshit to leave my mind. I'd never doubted us, or been suspicious of her, until five minutes ago. And it was only because of that fucking story. I knew Reagan. She wouldn't—Christ. I'd just told Brody that I wanted to marry her and wanted to be Parker's dad. He was right. Not even three months later and I was already thinking about *marrying* her? I couldn't do this. I just—I couldn't.

Reagan—*November 1, 2010*

PARKER'S FACE LIT up when there was a knock on the door, and I nodded my head in the direction of it.

"Tate," he finally choked out.

When he didn't say anything else, and all that met me was hard sobs, I asked, "She took him from you? How can she do that?"

"No!" he yelled, and a groan that didn't even sound human left him. "I killed him. I killed him—it's my fault—Tate's dead. Oh God, he's dead! I killed my son!"

I almost dropped the phone as I struggled to find my couch to sit down. This had to be some sick, twisted joke because of last night.

Right?

"Fuck!" he roared until more sobs choked off his words.

Wrong.

"What happened?" I finally managed to ask.

"I was driving, and he died. I don't—I don't—why couldn't it have been me?" he yelled, and somehow, I knew he wasn't asking me that question. "This can't be happening, he needs to be okay, I'll do anything. *Anything*, you hear me? God damn it! Take me instead!"

"Brody, no. No, I'm so sorry. God, when did this happen?" I asked when he'd been quiet a few minutes.

"Early this morning," he groaned. "Olivia sent me to the store, she said she just wanted some quiet time so I took Tate with me. It was icy, so fucking icy, so I was being careful. We were stopped at a red light, and the guy—the guy behind me couldn't stop." Brody didn't say anything else for a minute as more cries

filled the phone. "It pushed us out into the intersec-
tion and we got hit hard. I couldn't stop the car from
spinning—I swear to God I tried! I tried so damn
hard! It just wouldn't stop, I couldn't stop us. We hit a
median, but another car that had been trying to avoid
us swerved into us. I don't remember anything after
that until I woke up in an ambulance, and Tate—he
was—fuck! This isn't real, Steele! Tell me this isn't
fucking real! Tell me he's still alive."

"I'm sorry . . . I'm so sorry." I couldn't force anything else out. I couldn't believe this was happening
to him, I didn't know what to say to help him. I was in
shock and thinking the same thing. That this couldn't
be real. But the pain in his voice . . . you couldn't fake
that.

I listened to him break down harder than he had
the entire conversation, and tears filled my own eyes
when he continued to scream his son's name over and
over again. His son, who he'd fought so hard to be
able to see, who wasn't even a year old, who was taken
way too soon.

My chest ached for my friend, and my body
screamed at me to get Parker and hug him tight. To
keep him safe from anything that could possibly
happen to him.

I knew then that I'd made the wrong decision. That
I'd been quick to act on the first insecurity that popped
up—all because of some other guy's experience—and
had possibly ruined everything. I needed Reagan and
Parker. They were my family . . . my peace.

been home for a little over three months, you met her after I got home."

My head jerked back. "Yeah, I met her the day I got out, but that was the middle of August. That was—"

"Two and a half months ago." Saco was quiet while I sat there, not moving, not blinking. "So two and a half months, and you already want to marry her and adopt her son?"

I still wasn't saying anything. That couldn't be right.

"From what you've told me, and the stories I've heard from Hudson, Reagan's incredible. But slow down, you're twenty-four, she's twenty-two . . . just let this play out for a while. Make sure this is what you want first. Make sure you *want* to be a dad. I know you love them, but you don't want to make a decision now, regret it later, and break their hearts then. If it's meant to be, then it's not like either of you are going anywhere. So enjoy getting to know her before you marry her. You'll have the rest of your life with her and Parker."

"Yeah," I said on a breath, but I still couldn't believe what had felt like six . . . seven months with them was only two and a half. And still I wanted them to be mine. What was it Reagan had said to me in Hudson's apartment? *"Everything's fast with us, but fast feels right when I'm with you."* Never had truer words been spoken.

Scanning through the last dozen or so shots I'd just gotten, I nodded to myself and looked up at my client. "Those are gonna look great, man. If you wanted to change one more time, go for it."

It was only supposed to be an hour-long shoot, which is why I'd taken it when he called. And even though this is what I loved doing, I was glad the hour was almost up. I wanted to be with Reagan and Parker.

I walked over and started adjusting the lights while he changed, and glanced over my shoulder when I heard the side door to my studio open. My lips stretched into a wide grin when Reagan and Parker walked in.

Reagan's eyes widened, and an apologetic look crossed her face when she looked around. "I didn't know you had a shoot tonight."

"Last minute." I shrugged and pulled her in to kiss her quickly before hugging Parker. "Hey, bud! How was school?"

"It was good." He looked past me at my client and asked loudly, "Are you going to shoot him?"

Reagan looked horrified for all of a second before a sharp laugh burst from her chest, and it took everything in me to keep from laughing with her and my client.

Bending down, I got close to Parker's face and spoke softly. "Remember when I took pictures with him until he took a step back before looking back at the woman behind the window. "Lady, do not keep me from them right now," I said darkly. "Not after the phone call I just received. They need me, and I need to be back there. Now tell me. Where. Is. He."

She forcefully swallowed and straightened. "Room thirteen."

Pushing away from the counter, I walked quickly over to the doors and waited until I heard the beep before pulling them open and jogging through the crowded halls. Turning a corner, I saw a flag over a door with the number thirteen on it, and quickened my steps. Stepping in, I came to a stop when I saw Reagan talking with a doctor, and just past them was Parker, hooked up to too many machines.

I'd seen some of the worst things anyone could witness in this world—and, granted, I couldn't sleep from it—but seeing Parker lying in that bed was enough to make my knees go weak and all the air leave my lungs.

A short cry burst past Reagan's lips, and she launched herself into my arms.

"I'm here, baby," I managed to choke out as I pressed my lips to her head. "I'm here." Looking up at the doctor, I took a deep breath and steeled myself. It didn't matter how much it killed me to see Reagan break down, or to see Parker in that bed, they needed someone strong right now. "How is he?"

"Coen?" Parker mumbled, and I squeezed Reagan tighter to me. When she didn't react to it, I waited for the doctor to speak.

The doctor assessed the position I was in with Reagan, and figured it was fine to talk. "Good news is that even though there seemed to be a lot of blood, it was only because it was a head injury. The cut isn't big enough to require stitches even. We're waiting on the techs to come and take him back for X-rays so we can make sure there's no major swelling or any cracks on his skull. I don't know how much you know, but he was unconscious for a bit there. He's awake, but he feels nauseous and the lights are bothering him, so he's keeping his eyes closed. Typical of a concussion." He closed the folder and looked at me. "Do you have any questions?"

"Ray?" I asked quietly. When she shook her head, I moved us away from the door. "No."

"All right then, I'll be back once I have the scans. Techs should be in here any minute to take him back."

"Thank you."

I waited until he was out of the room and had shut the door before kissing the top of Reagan's head again, and pulling back. "You okay?"

Tears were still streaming down her face, but she nodded. "Yeah."

I tried to smile for her, but I wasn't sure if she bought it. "See? He's going to be fine. He's tough. Aren't you, bud?" I asked as I walked us closer to the bed and grabbed the hand that only had one wire coming off it.

"Because I eat my food," Parker slurred.